The
Coach

Jan Reed Bales

The Coach

Copyright 2018

Jan Reed Bales

Book Cover Design: D Baker Design

Editor: Kathy Jerore

ISBN-13: 978-1548080402

Acknowledgments

Would be authors are often told to write
what they know...

When I first thought about writing this book,
I found out I did not know much.

Through the years I gained knowledge and wisdom,
(I hope), so that I thought I was ready to put the book
down on paper.

First, acknowledgment goes to my family who collectively indulged me on many different levels.

Secondly, My best friend Bob Brnabic who through the years related his experience in Vietnam to which I used as a foundation for that part of the story. I was honored and humbled as Bob told his story. A true American Bad Ass.

Next would be my brothers who listened to sketches of the story I would tell as we shared lunches together.

And not last or least, I would like to thank Kathy Jerore who undertook the heavy task of editing and organizing my thoughts as I put them to paper.

CONTENTS

DEDICATION

To the real Hero's of the Vietnam War:

Our Brothers and Sisters in Arms

who never made it home.

Jan Reed Bales, Sp4

Chapter 1

SMITH PROJECTS
Detroit, Michigan, June, 1957

You are who you are now,
because of who you were then.

I was born in an Army camp hospital when my dad was in the service during the Second World War. So, I have a connection with the military that goes back to birth. I was named for a favorite Uncle whom I had never met. If everyone one has to have a name I had mine. So, Jack Tyler is it and after years of using it, I rather like the sound of it. Well, that is, until my Mom uses it to scold me. Every boy who has a mom knows the sound of his mom's voice when she calls. The worst sound is when she uses your middle name.

When your mom uses your middle name you are most likely in trouble, and my middle name got used a lot. I remember thinking as I hustled toward the house, what have I done now? The activities would flash in my mind and I would think Nah, she can not know I did that, or that, or that. But most of the time she knew. I guess I did not cover my tracks as well as I thought. However, life goes on, and mine certainly did. And God was about to gift me with another brother I would love forever.

Like most boys my age, life revolved around the things I liked to do, including those things that would get me in trouble from time to time. And like many young folks, I was able to talk my way out of some tough spots. Many of these tough spots were caused by my glib personality and need to be a smart ass to folks. In my neighborhood, it was not the best of ideas to smart off to the bigger kids. It also helped that I was fast on my feet and could outrun many of the kids. In addition, I learned real fast not to back down when given a challenge.

It's late Spring, early Summer, I am 12 years old and pretty much a regular kid who loves baseball and does not mind getting dirty. My family is living in Detroit in the Smith Projects near the streets of Lyndon and Evergreen in the Northwest area of Detroit, Michigan. And I have the world by the ass. The kids in the neighborhood are starting a new ball team to be sponsored by the Parks and Recreation Department of Detroit and we are going to hold an informal practice before we are broken down into teams by the Rec. Director.

It is in fact, my birthday and it's also my favorite time of the year because Spring means the Earth goes through its rebirth. The trees have budded out and the flowers and the fruit will soon follow. While at the park, I will check out the Mulberry and Pear trees. I can already taste the fruit from these trees. I looked up in a book to determine what type of pear tree is in the park. They are Bartlett pears.

I do know this; Bartlett pears are sweet and juicy. Many days, eating the fruit will be my only meal of the day unless I can collect a few coffee bottles or pop bottles to cash in. With that cash, I was able to buy a hamburger for dinner.

I have just finished rebuilding an old bike which I bought for $5 to use on my paper route. I'm on my way to play baseball with my buddies at Stoeple Park and to try out the bike.

Normally I would walk the two blocks to the park, but I just gotta see how the bike runs. An older friend and fellow newsboy helped me rebuild the bike. In return, I will deliver his paper route for free when he is too busy to do it. It was a fair trade in my book. A lot of the older guys were now buying cars so they would sell off their bikes and deals were pretty easy to get. I know I'm a bit young for a car, but I am thinking about learning to drive. One of the older guys who know how to drive, gives the younger guys driving lessons, for a price of course.

School only has a few more days till the end of the semester. That to me is always the best sign of summer. The lawns in the Rosedale Park area of Detroit will soon need cutting, and that means extra money for me. I know there are kids my age living in Rosedale, but for the life of me, I do not understand why we play ball on different teams. My thoughts are that if we combined our skills we would have a really great team. I have seen some of them play and they are not too bad. The team I will be on is made up from the kids from my school and the local Catholic school. However, the Catholic school has its own team in the CYO league and those guys cannot play with us until their season is over with. So today is kind of a practice of sorts.

Now the ball fields are drying out enough so that we can have a game without dodging mud puddles. As I approach the park, I can see some of the guys at the field already. They are just tossing the ball around. There doesn't seem to be enough guys for a decent game yet. I also know some of the guys are late sleepers and will show up as the games are going on. When I lean my bike up against the ball field backstop, I can see that Bob and Lou are already here. They are my best buddies from Harding and are in my class at school. Some of the guys gather around my bike and make comments about how nice it is. Mostly, they have smart ass remarks.

When I greet the guys, I see that there is a new face. A little guy, who is at least a half a head shorter than me standing by the backstop. So being the friendly guy that I am, I yelled at him "Hey, Shorty! Did you come to play ball or just watch?"

So the little guy yells back; "My name is Will. Not Shorty! And yes I did come to play ball. Do you have a spot for me?"

"OK Will. We have a spot for you. Can you play at all?"

"You bet I can. I love baseball!"

"Well you may love baseball but we'll find out how much baseball loves you."

"Great! You're on!"

"We'll choose up sides soon and you'll be able to play. We can always use another player."

As we played, I asked Will where did he live? "I live on Vaughan. We just moved in. We are right down the street from the Catholic Church."

Teasing him I asked; "So, you are one of the "rich kids" huh?"

"My Dad and Mom are not rich; they work hard for a living. Why would you say we are rich?"

"Because I live in the "Smith Projects" and so do most of the guys here. Most of us have never lived in a house like yours."

"What are projects?"

"Projects are those houses over there that are all connected together. They are owned by the city. Only poor families live in the projects. Families that have a lot of kids. Like mine."

"Oh? How many kids are in your family?"

"There are ten kids in my family. How does that sound?"

"It sounds like a lot of kids. I'm an only child."

"Yeah. It is a lot of kids, especially at dinner time. Okay, time to play ball."

So, now the games have begun. There was never enough for nine guys on a side. Mostly there would be five or six guys on a side. So we would play even up on the players and make the right field out. Meaning, If you hit a ball to right field, you would be out.

Another rule we used was that the pitcher's hand was out. If you hit the ball to the pitcher, or the ball was thrown to the pitcher before you reached first base, you were out. So that meant we did not need a first or second baseman. The batting team would also catch for the fielding team. Once the game began and I had a chance to bat at least once, the guys would complain that I hit the ball too far and too hard, so they made me switch to the left side of the plate.

I was a normal right-handed hitter, but when I switched, I had to bat left-handed. That meant I had to hit toward right field and that was considered out under our rules. So, I had to learn to hit the ball to the opposite field. After a while, I got so I hit equally well regardless, right or left handed.

I could tell after a few innings that Will was not a very good ball player, but he tried really hard and that was good enough for me. Will seemed to be able to catch and throw a ball well enough but he did not seem to know how to cover the bases and what to do when the ball was hit to him. Many times I had to coach Will on what bases to cover and to what bases he needed to throw the ball.

That day, like all the days that we played, we would play more than one ball game and most of the guys would take a break for lunch.

Bob and Lou knew that it was my birthday, so they both wished me a Happy Birthday before we quit for the day. Aside from sticking out my tongue at them, I just muttered thanks, smiled a little and just walked away.

On the following Monday at school, the Assistant Principal brought "Young, Mr. William Carter" into our classroom and introduced him to everyone. Our home-room teacher, Mr. Barr presented Will to all of us and asked if anyone had met Will yet?

My buddy Bob, or who I had thought was my buddy, piped up and said; "I think Jack knows William. He told me he met him over the weekend."

Mr. Barr looked at me and asked, "Jack, have you met William?"

"Yes, Sir," I said. "I met William over the weekend."

So it became my task to be sure "Young William" made it to his classes and lunch. All in all, it was not too bad. The biggest problem was the kids would ask me who my new little brother was and the girls would just snicker and point.

During our ball games that summer, it became evident that Will could catch a ball, and throw a ball, but could not hit very well. Seeing that he was the "new guy," my buddies always "let" Will be on my team.

So, I took the time to explain to Will some of the little things he could do to be a better hitter, like to watch the seams on the ball. By watching how the seams rotated, you may be able to tell if the ball was thrown hard, fast, or would it move off a straight line when it got close to the plate.

Will also had a problem of not being ready to swing when the ball was pitched. That may have been the hardest thing to teach him; how to hit a thrown ball. One thing Will could do well was run. He was easily the fastest runner of all the guys. Coach Carpenter switched Will to be a left-handed batter and after that Will became a great bunter and would get on base often and then he would steal second base and third base too.

The days ran on that summer, and Will and I became good buddies. I was surprised that he was the same age as me. I was 12 and Will was no bigger than a normal 10-year-old. And I was a little bigger than most 12-year-olds. Oh, and Will was touchy about being small.

Even though he was shorter than the rest of the guys, the girls did not seem to mind. Most of them would smile at him and make a point of saying; "Hello Will."

About 3 pm each day, I would leave the park to do my paper route. I was delivering the Detroit Times, and the rule was to have the papers delivered by 5pm, dinner time.

I loved being a paperboy. I earned good money and developed decent money skills. My dad had set down rules that $5 would go to my Mom each week to help pay for my keep. The rest was my profit. That meant I had about two or three bucks for me each week. Not a bad haul for a 12-year-old. I often invited Will to go with me on my paper route but he always said "No." Later I learned that he didn't know how to ride a bike and that his Mom would not let him cross the streets with his bike, even after he did learn to ride it. She worried he would get hit by a car.

I remember the first time I met Will's mom, Lois. She was a short, dark-haired lady who was very pretty. Will's dad Bill, had brown hair and was about the same height as my dad, 5'8". The more time I spent with Will, the more his parents trusted me as his friend. It was not uncommon for me to spend hours at Will's house when it was raining and we could not play ball. Will was also into reading and he always had a book to read in his room. For me, I was more into comic books and some adventure stories. Will did get me to read some of his books like Tom Sawyer.

By the end of the summer, Will's mom was letting him do more and more, including going with me on my paper route. Will's mom and dad would also ask me questions about how my paper route was going and how was I "building my business?"

The newspaper's station manager, Al Meyers, who worked for the Detroit Times, was more than fair to the carriers. However, he did not take any grief from us. One thing Al was a stickler for was paying your paper bill on time. He also made sure we kept our customer levels up. I started my route with about 65 customers and ended with over 100 when the Detroit Times went out of business in 1959.

At that time I was the youngest of the paper boys, and aside from Al, I relied on the older guys to teach me the ropes. The older carriers also helped Al keep the younger guys in line. Al taught me to ask the customers "How was the service this week?" Also, to ask if the customer wanted their paper delivered to a certain spot. All of those things would lead to more tips. He told me this was a way to gather information and satisfy your customers.

There were two times that were best to buy or sell a paper route. One time was at the beginning of the summer so the kids could have the summer off, and also right after Christmas when you had gotten all your tips. Many of the older guys would sell their routes when they graduated from high school. That was a great time to buy a good route.

My first route was subbing for Al on the Projects route. I did not have to do much except deliver the papers when Al had a day off. He also let me help him do collections as part of my training.

Al was making sure that I could handle a route on my own. About six months later I got my own route. My profits went up and so did my payments to my Mom.

In the summer I would do my route and return to the park to play some more ball afterward. Dinner for me was a hamburger or a hot dog on the go. Most times I got home just before dark. About 9pm. I sure put a lot of miles on my bike that summer.

Looking back now, I wonder how my mom let me have all of that freedom. I guess it was because I did not cause any problems, and she had all the other kids to worry about. My older brother Jay and I were pretty much on our own. My older sister stayed around the house and helped with the other kids. All in all, the kids helped each other, and my mom. Even with all the kids, there was never a problem to speak of. A true testament to my mom

Like all young boys my age, my mom was my first girlfriend. I remember telling her that I loved her and would marry her someday. She would tell me; "Jack, that's sweet, but someday you will meet a young lady who you will love more than me and you will marry her."

That summer, the Parks and Recreation Department of Detroit set up a baseball league for the kids in the neighborhoods. Some of the teams in the league came in as full teams and the other teams were made up of the extra players, like Will and I. One of the fathers pitched in and took over as a manager for our team. The kid's name was Rich and we all called his dad "Coach" or "Mr. Carpenter."

Mr. Carpenter taught us a lot of neat stuff we didn't know. He taught us stuff like pepper, infield, and outfield drills, and bunting. Rich was the catcher. I played shortstop, and Will played second base.

As kids, we certainly did not want to bunt, but we did learn how. Mr. Carpenter made sure we all learned the value of playing as a team and how the littlest of the efforts made could win a game.

We did not do well when we first started out, but we became better as the season went along. We ended up 8-7 and only won one game in the playoffs. Not a bad season for a bunch of misfits.

It was a learning experience for us to turn double plays and cover bases. Many of the things we did not need to do during our pick-up games. I remember that lots of times Will's mom would drop him off at the park with his lunch or sometimes with money to buy his lunch.

Our years as 13 and 14-year-olds were pretty much the same. A lot of baseball and delivering newspapers.

During that time, things did change for us. I took driving lessons from one of the older guys and was beginning to look around for a car.

My older brother kept reminding me about how young I was and asked me a question I could not answer. "Where are you going to park this rattletrap you're going to buy?"

Oh, And there was also a couple of other changes too. Will got a paper route and we discovered girls.

Chapter 2

WILL AND SHARON

We made it to the 8th grade at Harding Elementary School. For Will, there was never a doubt he would make it. But for some of us, it was a different story. I did okay in school. I passed the tests but failed to turn in much of my homework. I just could not find the time with working the paper route and a part-time job in the gas station. I had started working in the gas station kinda by accident. I would stop after my route and buy a pop and talk to the owner about cars.

One day when the station got real busy he asked me to pump some gas into a customer's car. His regular guy was off sick. I stuck around for the rest of the day and he paid me a couple of bucks. One of the things I would do was patch tires and drain off the excess oil left over from an oil sale. Back in those days, all cars burned oil and the drivers would get oil added as they filled up with gas.

Will and I would walk to school together most days, right up Lyndon to school. I began to wonder why

Will wanted to walk down Patton and cut up Kendall to the back side of the school. Then I realized, he timed his walk so he could say good morning to two girls, Sharon and Karen, who were sisters. I had thought that they were twins because they looked so much alike. But then I found out that Sharon was the older sister by one year. She was in the other 8th-grade class at Harding. I had seen her at school, but me being me, I didn't pay much attention to girls.

One day, I asked Will how he knew Sharon and Karen and he told me he had met them at his church. I asked him how he could tell them apart? He told me Sharon had a beauty mark under her chin on the right side and that Sharon was always in a good mood. Karen, however, was kind of a sourpuss.

When we met the girls on the way to school, Will asked me to talk to Karen so he could talk to Sharon. My response was; "Are you crazy? No way!" But, being the buddy that I was, I did try to keep Karen busy so the two "lovebirds" could talk. Yuk !!

Once at school, it would go back to just Will and I. At least during lunch Will did not insist on sitting with the girls, which was a good thing, because buddy or not I was not going to sit with girls during lunch.

Mr. Larson, the gym teacher at Harding, would tell us a day in advance if we were going outside to play ball. On those days, the guys would bring their ball gloves. But, it was softball and not hardball.

On other days, gym class was kickball and some other games. Some of the girls joined the boys and played too. I noticed that Will was always on the same team as Sharon. Many of the girls thought Will was a real cutie, but he was kinda short. Sharon didn't seem to mind.

After school, Will, Bob, and Lou would walk home together and tease the girls. Me? I did not. I had to hustle and deliver my paper route. Will did not have to hurry. He had sold his route, "to better use his time to study," so he said.

During the fall of our 8th grade, the school began having sock hops. Some of the kids from the other schools around Harding would also attend. It was at those dances that Will and Sharon were a real couple. Will would again ask me to keep Karen busy. So, I would usually keep her busy for about five minutes and then the other guys would pick up the slack. Karen seemed to like the other guys better than me anyway, and that was great in my book.

Many of the guys seemed to like Karen. All I knew was, I was off the hook. Some of the girls tried to get me to dance, but I really did not want to learn how. I did slow dance once in a while when I could pick out an older girl. I heard some of the girls saying that I was stuck up, but I guess I was really just shy.

After the dances, Will's mom, Lois, would come and get us to drive us home. On many of those nights, I would stay overnight at Will's. It was those evenings and the next morning that I would have a chance to talk to Will's mom and dad. I learned that Will's dad Bill, like my dad, had served in the military during World War II. Both Will's mom and dad were against all wars.

They said wars were a waste of good American boy's lives. They did think, however, that the United States had done the right thing during that war. I learned from Will's dad that he had been a Marine officer during World War II and had seen action in the Pacific. He had been wounded and that was why he had a slight limp.

Will's dad would sometimes ask me about my dad and where had he served during the war. I told him my dad was in the army in France and Germany. I also told him that my dad was 100% disabled and could not work. His disability was due to "shell shock." Will's dad seemed to know what shell shock was and he would shake his head, but I never heard him comment.

He told us a little about being in the Marines and some of the places he had been. He went to Guadalcanal, Tarawa and a few other places before he was wounded and sent home.

Bill told us that many of the soldiers had problems because of the war and because of the things that had happened to them during their service. He also said that some of the worse times were between the battles and not knowing where you would go next. Many times when battles ended you would go train and never really knew what the next mission was going to be. He told us the uncertainty was as bad as the battles.

Will's dad also told us of the times he was not able to change clothes for weeks at a time and how hot and dirty you could get just sitting around. Also, about the times you did not get a decent meal for weeks, and that rations were so scarce that the Marines would eat rice captured from the Japanese.

He told us that you would be very thirsty and yet you could not drink the water, because you would get sick. Many of the guys would set up tents to catch the rainwater and drink that and some of them still got sick.

One time I asked him if that was why he was always so neatly dressed and he laughed and said, "No, I just like to be neat. That was the way I was brought up. I need to be neat when I meet customers in the shop."

Bill would also talk to Will and me about the kind of work they did in the shop and how he had served as an apprenticeship when he was a young guy back in New York. He told us how he had met Will's mom when she had come into the shop as a billing and shipping clerk right out of high school.

Once I asked him why he joined the Marine Corp.

He laughed and said, "I did not join the Marine Corp, I was drafted and assigned to the Marines."

"If you were drafted," I asked, "how did you become an officer?" He told me he was what they called a "Mustang," a person who had worked his way up through the ranks. He told us that he had qualified for a deferment because he worked in the tool and die industry, but he had waved the deferment. I asked him if he was a hero? He looked at me and said; "Jack, the real heroes are the ones that do not come home."

"Jack," he told me, "it seems our country soon forgets the veterans and their sacrifices. Promise me that you will never forget those who have served. Both those who came home like your dad, and those heroes who never made it home."

Will's parents had bought a small tool & die shop in Detroit when the owner retired, and they had moved here from New York to see if they could be the keepers of their own future. The shop's products were mostly machining small items for bigger shops who did not want to do the smaller items. They also built small checking fixtures to check the quality of parts.

Chapter 3

HIGH SCHOOL YEARS
Detroit, Michigan

In the summer of 1960, Will and I left Harding behind and entered Redford High School. I was lucky in some regards. I had an older brother Jay and my older sister June, who were already attending the high school. I was a very busy guy. I had signed up for both freshman football and baseball. With football practice that fall, and my paper route plus a part-time job that I had at a local gas station, I did not have a lot of time for anything else.

My brother Jay had taken ROTC and I had planned on it too. Will's mom was against him taking it. One night, Will's dad sat us down and explained why Will's mom was against him taking ROTC. His parents did not want Will to get into a military mindset. They said that the military could become romantic to young people, with all the action and comradery that it offered. She was also adamant that Will should spend as much time as he could taking the higher math classes.

For me, ROTC was my favorite class. It offered structure, which I needed, and I wanted to do better than my brother had done. By the end of my first year, I had been promoted to Corporal. I volunteered for many of the details and began collecting the ribbons that indicated I had done the service. To me, the ribbons were cool.

During those high school years, both Will and I were very busy and the months and years seemed to fly by. I continued to take ROTC as a class and advanced through the ranks. I worked hard and was able to be on many of the teams like the rifle and drill teams. I also had qualified for a special summer camp for superior Cadets and I had a blast being on my own for the first time. Plus, for the first time, I paid attention to my school work and was promoted through the ranks.

Other classes were not hard for me, and I also spent a lot of time doing the required homework. I took the tests as required and kind of winged it when other things got in the way. I figured that if the baseball career didn't work out, I could join the army and make it a career.

Will and I also played on baseball teams outside of high school that was among the best in the Detroit area. It wasn't too long after that when Will and I started getting questions from the local colleges about playing in the future.

Will and I dove into high school activities and had a lot of friends. Will and Sharon continued to date. I, on the other hand, dated but I did not have a steady girl. We would double date for the drive-ins and dances. I seldom dated alone with just me and the girl. I was not a great talker so I could go hours without conversation. So in a way, I was not considered to be a very good date, but I was a great listener.

On weekends, while Will was working in the shop with his parents, I was working on cars. They were old clunkers, but I would fix them up and sell them to the other guys in the neighborhood. I had my own car before I had my license. It was an old 1949 Pontiac. I fixed a few rust spots on the body and used blankets to cover the seats. Because I had painted the spot that I had fixed with different colored primer, it didn't look that good. One young lady I dated refused to ride in it. I hope she enjoyed sitting at home that night.

As I began to save some money, I opened a savings account at a local bank. A few times I was able to give my mom some extra money for things needed around the house. It made me feel good that I could still contribute to the family in a small way.

During that time, while my brother Jay was in the Marine Corp. He would write home short, funny letters to the family. It was kind of a family thing to sit around and read them and laugh at the antics he and his buddy pulled on each other.

My sister got married to a friend of my brother and they were living close to my family. That left me the oldest kid at home. So, I was still mostly on my own, as always.

Sharon became like another sister to me and tried multiple times to fix me up with her girlfriends. She had finally given up on me dating her sister Karen. And to my benefit, Karen also had a steady guy, so once again I was off the hook.

In the summer, after the end of each school year, Will and I played travel baseball with many of the best players in the area. I hit for average but was more of a power hitter. Will, also a switch hitter, was a spray hitter too and could just about put the ball wherever he wanted. He was also very fast and was a threat to steal a base at any time. It was not uncommon for Will to get a single, steal second and wait for me to drive him in. Together we made a great team.

That summer, I also pitched a lot. All the guys that had decent arms and could find the plate did in a pinch. Will would catch a few innings to give the regular catcher a break. The pitching experience was good for me. I got to see how the pitchers and catchers sometimes set up the hitters. By the end of the summer, Will and I were getting attention from both colleges and professional teams. I really did not want to go to college. I felt I just wanted to be done with school. So, I needed to convince my parents to allow me to sign a baseball contract. The best offer I received was from the Chicago Cubs organization.

A number of offers came in and I talked them over with my parents and with Will's dad. The deciding factor for me was that in baseball, I would not have to go to classes anymore. So I signed a minor league contract with the Chicago Cubs organization.

Will had decided to attend college and become an engineer like his dad. So for the first time in years, Will and I would be separated. He at college and me starting out in my baseball career.

Chapter 4

LIVING THE DREAM

The following year I was playing baseball in the low minors for the Chicago Cubs and enjoying every minute I was there. The stadium we were playing at was great and the fans provided a lot of support for us. Many of the fans would volunteer to help with the upkeep of the stadium and field. I was living with a local couple to reduce living costs and was also able to save a few extra bucks here and there. The couple treated the younger guys like me as sons. Many were empty nesters and got joy having us wild young guys around. But, they did have house rules. One of them being: NO overnight guests.

My big chance to move up a class/league came when one of the journeyman players moved up to the parent club because of an injury to the starting third baseman. At that point, I was moved up to the Iowa Club. It was somewhat of a mystery to me as to why I was the one moved up from the A-Ball team to the Double-A team because there were other players in the organization that was in line ahead of me. I had only been in the organization for two years and I was just a few months into my second season and not one of the "chosen few," considered to be a favorite of the parent club.

Of course, I was hoping they moved me up because they thought I had a good chance to make it into the "Big Club". The Club was mum about why I was moved up. Their comment was "Just pay attention to your job and it will all take care of itself. And just have fun" In the clubhouse, many of the younger players like me "practiced" being General Manager by trying to determine who, why, how the next guy would be "the guy" to move up. Most of the time we were totally wrong.

In the process of playing, I was learning things about the game I had never heard of before; cut off plays, coverage plays, and offensive signals. Many times I thought that I was doing poorly and would ask the coaches about my progress. If I heard it once, I heard it a thousand times; "Jack, you have all the talent in the world, but if you cannot get your head out of your ass, you'll never see the show. " So most of the time I kept my head out of my butt and into the sunshine.

The team moved me from shortstop to third base. The coaches and manager explained that I did not have the range of a major league shortstop, BUT, I did as a third baseman. I continued to switch hit and I became a much better hitter after listening to and learning from the hitting coaches. During the year, as I became more aware of the league, the pitchers and what was expected of me, my hitting improved to where I was well over .300 and with increased power. I was now having more fun. I was driving the ball to all fields and would at times try to see if I could place the ball right where I wanted too. I was careful though to not play the game within the game, unless the timing was right.

Eventually, they moved me up to second in the batting order, and that meant my bunting opportunities during the course of a game increased. My "at bats" against the better pitchers also increased.

Early one morning during practice, the manager called me into his office and explained that the Club had gotten an emergency phone call from my mom. They told me I had to call home immediately. "Like now! Use this phone right here" they told me. So, I called my mom only to find out that I had gotten a draft notice. She told me she knew it was a draft notice because many of the other guys in the neighborhood who were my age had also gotten their notices in the past few months.

My mom opened the letter to me, so she could see what my report date would be. The letter said I had to report for a physical in two weeks. I asked my mom to send the letter to me via air mail. I needed to see the letter and the ball club needed to have a record of it so they could provide me a leave of absence from the club. They said they could request a deferment and that I could join the Iowa National Guard and fulfill my obligation that way. After much discussion and hand-wringing, I decided to just go with the notice and see where things ended up. There was always a chance of not passing the tests.

The next week was kind of a blur. I played ball, but not very well. When the letter got there we had a conference and the club told me to take a few days off and to go home early. They also wanted me to keep them in the loop about what was happening.

So I took a few days, hopped a plane and went to Detroit for a visit. Will was away at college and most of the other guys had been drafted, enlisted or were working. I guess Uncle Sam was cleaning out the neighborhood. The word in the Smith Projects was that almost all of the guy's age 20 to 24 were getting their draft notices and notices to report for induction physicals.

Will was not home at the time because he was away at college, I at least got together with his parents and set up a trip with them to go and see him on campus. Will, his parents and I spent most of the day just goofing off and talking about old times.

Will had signed up for Navy ROTC in college to lessen his college tuition. His parents were not overjoyed with the ROTC decision but true to form, they did not voice their objections to Will and let him make his own decisions. Will was doing rather well in ROTC and had qualified for flight school. Needless to say, I was very proud of my little buddy.

Will was also playing baseball. The coach had converted him to catcher and Will said he loved it. He was now in the center of all the action.

Another thing caught my eye. Will was now 5'10" and he had filled out to nearly 160 pounds and solid as a rock. He laughingly kidded me that he had to keep his weight down if he was going to fly fighters. Will was taking ground training at the time.

It was soon time to leave for home so we gave each other big hugs, said our goodbyes, and I got into his parent's car for the long ride home.

While I was home, I stopped at the shop to say "hello" to Sharon. She looked great. I guess being over 21 for a lady was not such a bad deal.

My time at home prior to my physical went quickly. I spent the time with my older brother Jay, and the rest of my family. My brother would kid me and tell me 10 times a day, "Don't go outside the wire." When I asked him what he meant, he would just laugh and slapped me on the back. My brother had already spent two tours in Vietnam and came home to work in the tool shop for Will's dad. What I remembered about my brother was his jovial nature. Plus, his laugh and his smile were the same as it was before he left for the service. So, I guess the Corp. had not changed him too much.

When I got home from Iowa, I also met up with some of my old buddies. One of them, named Jimmy, had gone for his physical just a few days before and gave me the lowdown on what to expect. Some of the older guys had passed along some tales of their induction. If I could, I should avoid being the fourth guy or the eighth guy in line. It seemed that every fourth guy was drafted into the Marine Corp.

On the day of the physical, my friend Jimmy drove me down to Fort Wayne in Detroit. I was surprised at how quiet it was there at Fort Wayne. Aside from the shuffling of feet as the guys moved from room to room and the directions being given by the military, no one was talking. The actual physical was not as complete as the one I had gotten from the ball team prior to my signing my contract nearly three years ago. I had always prided myself in being in great physical shape, now I wasn't too sure if it was a plus or minus.

As luck would have it, I passed the physical. I also got directions on when to report for my induction and was told to be ready to ship out that same day. When I got back to my mom's I called the ball club and gave them an update.

Chapter 5

NIGHTMARES ARE ALSO DREAMS

My induction date was set for two weeks, which was one day after my 21st birthday. So, I guess a beer party with my buddies was not gonna happen. Besides many of them had already gone into the military. My brother Jay told me what I would need to take with me. He also told me "do not take anything you want to keep, and if you wanted to send things home you would need to pay the postage yourself." He told me to plan on giving the stuff to charity or just toss it away. He also said to take shaving gear, toothbrushes, soap, and a wash rag and towel. Also, I should be prepared to toss away any clothes that I take with me. "Your wonderful Uncle Sam would provide you with new duds." Then he laughed.

On the day of my induction, they re-took our fingerprints. A couple of Marine Sgts. came into the room and asked if anyone wanted to join the Marine Corp? There were a few guys that raised their hands and they were led off into another room.

Then they had us assemble in a large room in a rough formation and swore us all in at once. After that, they had us count off by fours. It was then that I remembered not to be the fourth, or eighth guy. At that point, I couldn't switch if I had wanted to. But, it turned out that I was number nine. Lucky me, I guess.

Welcome to the US Army. And just as my friend Jimmy had told me, every fourth guy was now a US Marine. The Marines were then taken to another room. One of the guys joked that they were going to get their first beating. Then I remembered, some of the other advice my brother had given me, like; "No sense making friends. You never know where you will end up." I was beginning to think that my brother Jay was wise beyond his years.

We were told we could call home, but we could not leave the post, nor were we allowed to have visitors. Some of the guys called home and asked their families to bring them clothes and supplies for three days. As it worked out we would be leaving later that night for Fort Knox, Kentucky. Being a ballplayer and used to traveling, I knew how to pack. My kit bag was stuffed with candy bars, bottles of pop, underwear, extra socks, the towel, washcloth, and the other items Jay had said to bring I knew I may need enough for the three days that we would spend in the reception center. Later that evening, we were fed good, old government chow. Not too bad, is what I thought.

Around 10 pm that evening we were loaded onto buses and driven to the train station. One of the Army Sergeants came around and told us to try to get some sleep on the train. He said we were on our way to Fort Knox, Kentucky, and we would not arrive till early the next morning.

Somehow, we did manage to sleep. When we were wakened up, it was near daylight. They got us off the trains and into a large area where we ate breakfast. I heard the guys asking if we were in Kentucky yet. I let it slip that we were in Cincinnati, Ohio. I had played a few games there against the local minor league team and I remembered the hills that had surrounded the area. After breakfast, they herded us back onto the train. I noticed the army was calling roll and checking our names off the master list. Not much later after that, we arrived at what was to be our new home, Fort Knox.

Back onto buses, again. We were driven to the "Reception Center'" and were told that we would be staying there for the next few days. We were also told to call home and let our families know that we had arrived safely. So more than 200 G.I.'s lined up to make their calls home.

My parents did not have a phone at home so I called my brother at the shop where he worked. I knew he would pass along the message to the family. He told me to be sure to drop a postcard in the mail as soon as I got assigned my Basic Training outfit. Then the Sergeant broke us down by last names into groups of sixty people and assigned us to barracks where we would stay for the next few days.

After we found a place to bunk, we were called out to the company area and told to get ready for chow. A regular army Private came over to lead the way. For many, it was their first experience of marching in a group.

The same private came in later that evening and read off a list of eight names. Those guys would be the new KP's for tomorrow's mess hall duty. Lucky me, I was number six. That's when I remembered my dad telling me to "never argue with a cook."

We spent the next few days in the new recruit reception area of Fort Knox. Some of the guys were pulled out of the platoon and some new guys took their place. In the process, we went to the Supply Depot and were fitted with uniforms, boots and the other items required to complete basic training. Then we marched to the barber shop to get a haircut, or more correctly, have all of the hair on our heads shaved off.

After chow, we went down to the local PX, signed a pay voucher for $10. All of us bought identical razors, shaving soap, bath soap with a soap container, toothbrush, toothpaste, a comb and a lock for our footlocker. It was what the army called the "Flying 10" because added up, all the items that we just signed for, came to ten bucks.

Note: to this day, I did not know what we were going to use a comb for. Our hair was never longer than our eyebrows. I also bought some baby oil for my new boots. Some of the guys also bought cigarettes and candy. We were marched back to the company area and the barracks. Then we were told to get rid of any of our civilian clothes and any other items brought from home. My brother Jay had been spot on.

The following morning we were lined up by height. Because I was nearly 6'2" I was the second guy in the first row. Then as our names were called, I was now Pvt. Tyler, we went to another position where we were instructed to stand on white squares painted on the ground.

Through the day we were given a number of shots by the medics. One of the medics was a guy from the neighborhood and one I had played ball with. I remember, he had asked if I was still into baseball and I told him, "I was until I was drafted". I was assigned Fourth Platoon, as my last name was in the T to Z group. I was positioned near the front of the platoon. After our company was fully formed, we were then marched to our new company area. It was the area where we would be stationed for the duration of our "Basic Training."

The Training Specialist 4th class was a tall, lean man named Pierce. He got us all together and told us to find a bunk, a footlocker and get all of our gear put away. He also told us to be out in the company area in platoon formation at 1600 (4 pm).

I selected a bunk on the first floor at the end of a row. That way, I would only have one person next to me and have the extra space.

At 1350, (1:50 pm) I went outdoors and located the space we would use for First Platoon. Some of the other soldiers were already there so I asked if any of them knew what was next. The response I got was negative shakes of the head. So, because of the training, I had in High School, ROTC, I began to organize the group into a rough platoon formation. I was just about finished when Sp. Pierce showed up. Pierce shouted; "As you were! Who positioned you a** holes like this?" I stepped forward and said, "I did Sp. Pierce."

"Well, carry on private. Let's see what you got." So, I continued to get the platoon organized. As I did, I explained to the soldiers what I was doing and why. I taught them to Dress Right, Dress, and other basic commands. Once we were organized, Pierce had me take up the Platoon Guide position and we marched over to the mess hall for chow.

Basic Training was easy for me. I was in top physical shape (from baseball training) and had done nearly all of the basic dismounted drills during high school and while at a summer camp that I had qualified for during high school. The weapons were also a repeat of the lessons learned in high school ROTC.

Sp. Pierce took me aside and had me begin the dismounted drills for the platoon. He told me he was not going to be our Training Sergeant but would be Assistant to S. Sgt. Jones who was on leave for the next week. Pierce also had me wear an armband with Sgt. stripes on it, denoting me as the Platoon Guide. He told me that S. Sgt. Jones may select someone else when he returned, but for now, I was it.

My duties as platoon guide included making sure all the guys were in the barracks each night and that the fire guards were assigned. Fire guards were on two-hour shifts and served as the lookout for any fires or potential fires. In the mornings I made sure the platoon was formed for training. I would also march the platoon from area to area.

Later, I found out that Pierce did not have any training experience. He had spent the majority of his enlistment as an Honor Guard. He had decided to change his occupation and chose to be a Training Sgt. So basically, he was in training just as we were. Since I had the experience of training high school students, he and I made a decent team. Pierce left all of the drill training and marching the platoon from location to location up to me.

It was my responsibility to teach the platoon how to field strip their weapons, shine their boots, make their bunks, and many other background things not normally covered during basic training. I also taught the guys some tricks on how to clean a rifle without busting their asses. It was a trick my dad taught me after we went small game hunting.

The trick was to break down your weapon into smaller pieces and use hot boiling water to get rid of grease, oil or dirt. Then you applied a light coat of oil and you were done. In addition, I instructed the guys how to soften up their boots by using baby oil in the spot that needed to bend while walking or running. The guys seemed to appreciate the extra tips and generally followed my lead.

There was only a problem with one young guy from Tennessee. He seemed to resent the fact he needed to get out of the rack in the morning along with the rest of the guys. He kept at me as to how he was going to kick my ass as soon as I didn't have my strips on. But being the project kid that I was, and having grown up fighting with all the kids in the neighborhood, I gave him his opportunity one evening after chow.

The guys in the barracks cleared out space on the second floor and I invited my friend to "take his best shot." He got in a few swings which I blocked with my arms and shoulders and floored him with a sharp left jab when he tried a "roundhouse right." It was over in less than a minute. And that little dust-up seemed to elevate my status with the rest of the guys.

When S. Sgt. Jones returned from leave, he and I had a discussion and he kept me on as Platoon Guide. He told me he had discussed my demeanor and skills with the other Platoon Sgts. in the company. They told him that I had done a passable job.

During a basic records check, the army discovered I had won a National Award in high school that qualified me to enter the military at the rank of Private First Class. (PFC E-3). S. Sgt Jones insisted that I wear the stripes, so I did. Then I was assigned a Cadre Room to be my bedroom. I was a "Happy Camper," well sort of. As happy as I could be under the circumstances.

All new recruits went through a series of testing. There were many college graduates in our company who were also draftees, so I figured I'd be down near the bottom. S. Sgt Jones explained it was more of an aptitude test and was not competitive to the other guys. The test was more of an IQ test, with logic tossed in for grins.

Again, I must have done well because a few days later I was called into the Orderly Room for a conference with the Company Commander. He told me I qualified for entrance into the Military Academy at West Point, and did I want to go on the special enlisted man program? I was adamant that I did not want to go. I told him that I already had a career path with baseball and that I would do my two years and say "goodbye" to the Army.

My second choice was to attend OCS, (Officers Candidate School), but again it required me to sign up for an extension of my military enlistment. Again I said "No." Then, I was "Ordered" to attend NCO School after Basic and learn to be a "Non-Commissioned Officer" and there was no discussion. That was to be my next assignment!

Seven other guys from our company were also assigned to the school and three others went to the Commissioned Officers school to become Officers. They all had to sign up for the additional service time.

I passed the NCO course with no problem, and I was promoted to the rank of Sgt. E-5. Later I was assigned to the advanced infantry school at Scofield Barracks in Hawaii. There, we went through very intense jungle training, search and rescue training, and we did not have any doubts as to where we were going when we completed our training. One of the classes we took involved a complete weapons training. I was selected to use an M-60 machine gun.

After duty hours, I would sometimes head for the Minor League facilities and hit and do some light fielding. I was also able to keep in touch with the Cubs Organization via the other clubs telephone network. One of the older baseball coaches named Bill Curry, who was an Army Veteran of the Korean War, told me just before we shipped out "Kid, don't go outside the wire." That brought back memories of what my brother had said. I think I knew what he meant, however, I was still not quite sure.

After we completed our training we were given leave. We had two weeks to go home and then return to Hawaii to await further orders. Prior to Leave, we all received a lot of shots. We didn't ask what they were for. We all knew where we were headed.

Once again the school was not difficult and near the end, I was asked if I wanted to attend Ranger School or Jump School. I declined because they would also require an extension of my military time.

It took nearly five days back and forth in travel time but I really enjoyed my time at home. Jay was engaged and was planning his wedding in a few months. I knew it would be one I would miss.

Will and Sharon had gotten married, to the surprise of everyone, except for Will's mom, Lois. Will was then off to Flight Training in Florida and I was saddened that we could not be able to get together before we both had to ship out.

In some ways, it was a good and a bad visit. A lot of things had changed in just a short amount of time since I was gone. There were reports of some of the older guys who had died in Vietnam and a few reports of some of the local guys being in the VA hospital in Allen Park, Michigan. Many of the younger guys were in the service, having joined the Navy and Air Force. Bob had joined the Navy and Lou, the Air Force. Both had done the wiser thing than I and didn't wait for the draft. Not too many of the guys joined the Army or the Marines. Go figure! Prior to leaving, Jay took me aside, gave me a big hug and told me to come home safe.

Chapter 6

DA NANG, SOUTH VIETNAM
In Country

Prior to shipping out of Hawaii, we updated our "Last Will and Testament." Here's where I ran into a problem. I thought about having my mom as my beneficiary, then thought better of it because I figured it would be too much of a burden on her if something happened to me. So, I decided to put Will's mom and listed her as my Aunt. I also listed my brother Jay as the second contact and gave the phone number of the shop as the contact phone number.

Three days after we returned to Hawaii, we were in transit to South Vietnam. We arrived in Da Nang at night. We were all very tired, but not many of us slept. We were just too geared up.

At the airport where we landed, was a beehive of activity. It was difficult to believe it was the middle of the night. People and machines were going everywhere. I figured even if we had a place to sleep we could not. There was way too much noise. We were led to a common area inside an air hanger where we could use the head (lavatory) and ate chow, which was not very good chow. Then we were led to a spot in the rear that would be our "area" for the next few days.

Early the next morning, the Company Officers and Senior Non-Com's had a meeting to discuss our trip to the Base Camp, which would be our home for the next 13 months. The Senior NCO's called the Junior NCO's together and briefed us on the Order of March which would be in a few days. They were joined by some additional NCO's from the Base Camp that we were going to occupy. The NCO's went over the nuances of the camp and the surrounding area.

The old man of our company, First Sergeant Mike Wilson, (we called him Iron Mike), gave us a little pep talk. We all paid rapt attention. Top Sgt. Wilson was a WW2 Veteran and had done multiple tours in Vietnam. Top said "Guys remember you are in a combat area where anything can be a danger to you and your fellow G.I.'s. There are snakes, rats and other animals that can kill as dead as the VC. "This is a place where you can trust no one, but the guy next to you. Have a good tour, and get out of here and back home safely."

I thought Iron Mike had said pretty much what the rest of us had been thinking since the beginning of our jungle training in Hawaii. Iron Mike had said a lot in just those few short sentences. A few days later as nightfall was approaching, our company loaded into trucks and proceeded up Highway 1 toward our Base Camp. The plan was to arrive early morning, then we would have all day to get settled, and get acquainted with the surrounding area. Not many of the guys talked above a whisper.

One thing I remembered was it was very dark. The lights of the trucks were on blackout mode but the stars added a little light. I was sitting in the third truck with my squad. It must have been early morning because I had dozed off with my chin hitting my chest from time to time. I do not know how long I had slept, but I was awakened by a loud explosion. I remember thinking; "What the hell?" as I got the sleepiness from my mind and remembered where I was.

The noise had come from the front of the convoy where the IED (Improvised Explosive Devise) sappers were riding. I quickly ordered my squad out of the truck and to take up positions on the right side of the truck. We, the squad leaders had been assigned to muster to one side of the convoy, my side was the right side. I ordered them not to fire unless we took fire on our position. I also told them not to talk and no one was to use any lighters or, cigarettes and to keep the noise to a minimum.

Within a few minutes, a runner came back to report that the first truck had run over an IED, and some of the other guys in the company were hurt really bad. We were told to hold position and have the medic go to the front of the column. I sent up the medic.

A few minutes later, we could hear helicopters approaching. There turned out to be three incoming. My squad was ordered to provide cover for the LZ, (landing zone), and standby for the evacuation of the casualties.

The odd thing was many of the guys were smokers, but they knew better than to light up. I knew a few of them chewed so they passed around their pouches to the other guys. I smiled at that because I knew from my baseball days, that some guys would likely get sick.

I could hear some of the guys whispering back and forth. One guy said; "Welcome to the country of Vietnam. Your home for the next 13 months." At that point, I ordered silence and assigned a watch with a rotation so the guys could get some sleep. Our base camp was situated atop a small hill that was 521 feet above sea level. It was named Camp 521. The camp was surrounded by rings of barbed wire and contained range markers.

Due to the delay, we did not arrive at base camp till early afternoon. We were greeted by some of the Non-Com's we had met a few days ago and some other holdover personnel that would be around for a few weeks to help us make the transition at 521. The Senior NCO's got busy and assigned us to our bunkers and "suggested" to us a logical sleeping arrangement. I was told be ready for a briefing at 1630. We received our assignment to patrol and protect Highway 1, from the VC (Viet Cong) and the NVA, (North Vietnamese Army).

We spent a great deal of time on patrol "outside the wire." There were different routes we would follow. We did not keep a regular schedule and we varied which route, the times and the days we would "do the rounds." There were also a number of villages in our area and we would stop and talk to the elders to determine where the VC were located and what the VC was up too. We did not get a lot of info though; because the villagers knew if they spoke to us, they would be punished by the VC.

We were told that at one time, the villagers were more cooperative, but the VC were vicious in their punishment. Even little kids were shy about accepting candy from us. We were told that there were some areas we should not enter. Those areas were mined and booby-trapped, so we tended to avoid those places. The officers had discussed doing a "house cleaning" of those areas, but the higher up brass did not want to commit the resources.

The order of march for the patrol fell into an orderly formation. We became more self-sufficient and relied less and less on the holdovers. During the earlier patrols, the holdovers evaluated the guys to determine their skill levels, such as advanced scouting. We began to refer to the holdovers as "oldies" although many of them were younger than us.

Some of the fellows in our company were great scouts while others were not. The "not's" were no less the soldiers, but they did lack the knack of noticing all the nuances of a patrol area. My normal spot in the patrol formation was near the front. I carried an M-60 machine gun and I could lay down a lot of rounds in just a few seconds. At times I would be the Senior Non-Com on the shorter patrols. At those times, the thought that I was responsible for my fellow soldiers was stressful. It was during those times I relied on the training I learned at the NCO school and the lessons by the holdovers. In addition, much of what we did and did not do was common sense. We were all growing up in a hurry.

Every once in a while we would come across caches of weapons that the VC had hidden in the jungle. Other times we would get into small firefights, but the VC seemed to blend back into the jungle and stop contact. We picked up a few wounds and the guys would be transported by medevac to the rear and most returned within a few days.

We did learn that while being outside the wire on patrol, some items we carried would be more important than others. I never left base camp without as much water and ammo than I could carry. I took a few changes of socks and one change of underwear. I would wear the same uniform for the entire patrol, be it two days or two weeks long. Many times I would throw away the underwear that had become rags while on the patrol. We were hesitant to toss out the ragged uniforms though. It may be a long period of time to get replacements.

As a company, we fell into a routine at base camp and at times we were bored. I continually told my guys; "if you get bored, clean your weapons, clean your clothes and secure our bunker." For the most part, Camp 521 was injury free. The days passed into weeks and months and we fell into a routine that was not all peaches and cream but was not at all bad either.

Some of the fellows handled the tension and stress better than some of the others. But all in all, we kept at it. One of the highlights would be the days the mail arrived. We would sit around with our close friends read the letters and pass out any goodies we received from home. We found out early in the tour that the goodies would be eaten by the local bugs and animals, so it was better to just give them away. Pictures from home were the best gifts. It showed us that folks at home were living okay, and maybe, just maybe we were here doing some good.

It was near midnight, just six days from our company's outward rotation to return back to the States, that we came under attack once again. Our sentries were on guard. The dogs and their handlers were doing a normal walk around when "all Hell broke loose!"

There was an immediate barrage of rockets slamming into our base camp, followed by heavy small arms fire. We hit the floor with the first blast as the bunker shook to its foundation. The guys in our dugout grabbed whatever we could and hit the door running.

As we hit the door opening, we were met with increased fire. It was as if the enemy was waiting for us to emerge. It was fortunate for us that our door opening faced toward the center of the camp and not toward the outside wire. As we scooted and half crawled to our battle stations, the rocket fire also increased. There were 10 soldiers assigned to our bunker and all of us made it out the door.

Once we were at our stations, the mortar rounds began to drop into the area that we occupied. The enemy seemed to have zeroed in on us. I could hear the guys taking wounds, mostly by the screams and grunts. At times you could hear the rounds whizzing by and feel the heat. We were doing our best to lay down as much fire as we could. There was a lot of noise, screaming and other activities that added to the general chaos.

Through the battle, I could see why the Senior NCO's were the true leaders in the military. For the most part, they were calm and provided the leadership and glue to hold us all together. A few of them were real old timers. Hold over's from WWII. Some were older than my dad. The Senior NCO's would move from position to position and instruct us how to better fight off the attack and to protect ourselves.

A brief thought hit me that the battle also had a horrible smell. Aside from the gunpowder, there was the smell of human waste and the odor of sweat, both from fear and exertion. The medics were running from post to post-treating those that they could. I had a thought that I hoped no one would fire at one of our own medics. The medics told us during previous drills, that they would enter from a certain area. All in all, that held true. How the medics kept their wits about them was a mystery to me, even to this day.

One of my squad members noticed that a contingent of the enemy was advancing on an adjoining position in mass. Due to the fact we were in the on top of a hill dug into trenches, we could see the advance. The VC had knocked out the fire team and had advanced to the outer ring of our parameter. A few of us slid out of our position toward the advancing VC and began to lay down as much fire as we could to hold back their advance. Once our mortar crew got set up, they were able to drop multiple rounds into the enemy positions.

When we first arrived at the base camp, we had been schooled as to what the range markers denoting distances to the target. Those markers were invaluable to our gun crews. My loader and I set up the machine gun and began firing. We noticed that the advance finally seemed to be losing steam and it was at that moment that I lost consciousness.

Chapter 7

GREAT LAKES NAVAL HOSPITAL

When I got back states side from Vietnam, I was a mess. When I finally awoke I had no clue where I was and I was not even sure who I was. My left leg had a few holes in it, caused by both bullets and shrapnel. It was the same with my back which was also riddled with too many pieces of shrapnel to even count. I knew I had to have been hit by shrapnel, although I had no recollection at that point of how I had acquired it. I also found out that I had no vision in my left eye, and I was wearing an eye patch. Waking up was very hard to do. In fact, waking up was a long, hard and painful ordeal. It seemed to take forever, but in reality, it was only over a period of a few days. Recovery though would take a lot longer.

Finally, I realized I was in the military hospital. Where exactly, I did not know. I was later told I was at Great Lakes, Illinois. All the above was learned two weeks after I awoke from a 16-day coma. It is difficult to even now to recall much of my life from the moment we came under attack at our base camp in Vietnam. It wasn't until years later that I learned what really happened at the base camp that night. I was told that as we took up our new downhill positions that we got hit by an RPG (rocket-propelled grenade). The remainder of the fellows were able to fight off the attack. But not without the company losing eight brave Americans, and with countless others wounded. The total time of the attack lasted less than 15 minutes. It was those brief 15 minutes that would change my life forever and end the life of many of my friends.

After regaining some of my senses, it began to dawn on me that I was no longer "n country." The staff was less hurried and they seemed to want me to fully engage. What seemed like many days of being in and out of consciousness, in reality, was just a few days. I did notice that something was interfering with my left eye. I spent considerable time trying to rub the sleepers out of my eye. One of the nurses, who I learned to recognize because she had red hair would tell me "Sgt. Tyler, I order you to stop rubbing your eyes or I will tie your hands to the side of the bed."

About the fifth day, a Doctor Paulson came into my room after I awoke and he began the slow process of explaining to me what injuries I had. I still remember his first words. "Sgt., I was not sure if we would ever have this conversation. You are pretty beat up." And with that being said, I fell back to sleep.

During the next few days, I was able to stay awake for longer periods of time and became more aware of my circumstances, both physically and mentally. I remember looking in the mirror and did not even realize it was me that I was looking at. I had lost about 30 pounds and was gaunt and very thin and still had the remaining blackness under my eyes. I remember thinking I could go out begging for Halloween as a zombie. But one thing I was looking forward to was to be able to go to the bathroom on my own and not have to use that bedpan. Plus, being able to eat some solid food again. It had been a while since I was able to have a decent meal. Counting the year I had spent in Vietnam it was over a year since I had a really good meal.

The United States Army had determined that I required physical therapy for recovery and to become a valued citizen again. Physical therapy was slow going. The eye patch came off, but the vision was still a problem. I could sense movement to my left, but I could not tell what was moving. The doctor told me that I may or may not gain the vision that I had lost. But, my biggest worry was; would I be able to see well enough to play baseball again?

Part of the eye therapy was to wear a patch over the right eye to see if the left eye would regain some of its strength. The therapy helped some, but the left eye became fuzzy when I was looking forward.

The leg also posed a problem. The docs patched up the wounds and repaired the calf muscle as best they could. I learned how to maneuver around with crutches and got really good with them. After about five weeks I progressed to a cane. Taking small steps. It was a time of reflection for me. Thoughts of my old plans passed before me and the future did not look good. Baseball as a career seemed to be way off in the distance. My moods went from happy to be alive and then to; why did this happen to me?

Sharon and my mom wrote to me and I called home to the tool shop when the mood would strike me. Sharon kept me abreast of what was going on with Will. He was flying jets off of a carrier in Vietnam.

Will and Sharon now had a son, born just days after Will had shipped out to the Gulf of Tonkin, off the coast of Vietnam. They told me they named him "William Jack" after his dad and I. I cried that night thinking that someone loved me enough to name their child after me. Sharon kidded me by saying that I was probably going to be an old bachelor anyway and it may be my last chance for a namesake.

The care at Great Lakes, I have to admit was wonderful. Plus there were a number of really cute, young nurses aids that helped us with anything we needed. Some of the guys really fell for a sweetie named Edwina. She was a redhead with green eyes and was from Texas, and she had that sweet Texas drawl.

The younger guys nicknamed me "The Pirate," because of my limp and the eye patch, plus the fact I would skip shaving for a few days at a time. Edwina quite often offered to shave me and I finally did let her do that once. Then gave up. I thought her time was more valuable spent elsewhere assisting the other guys who needed more care than I did at that point.

Seeing I was in the Chicago area, the Cubs sent representatives over to monitor my progress and to try to determine my future in baseball. I spoke with the Cubs and told them that I would be ready to attend training in the Spring, which was only five months away. I was just 22 years old. Close to the age of the kids that came out of college to play ball.

Christmas came and went and I spent my time in the hospital slowly recovering my balance and my eyesight. Although I had always been a loner at heart, it was a difficult season for me to be away from family and friends. I often reflected about playing ball with my buddies and how I missed the small things we would do to have fun during the holidays.

Then, if things weren't bad enough, right after the New Year, I was called to the message center to pick up an urgent message from home. It was from my brother Jay. He wanted me to call him ASAP.

There are times, even to this day, when I wished I had never gotten that message. And there were days

I also wished time and again, that I had not made it home from Vietnam. When I called Jay at the shop, he told me that Will had been shot down in Vietnam. He explained that Will had been flying a close air-ground support mission in the south and had been hit by multiple small arms fire and rockets. The Navy asked the Mud Marines to provide a search and rescue mission at the crash site and fortunately, they were able to recover Will's remains. The Marines had to fight their way into the site and called Huey's in to do the evacuation. At that time, I was nearly 23 years old. Will would never be older than 23.

When I heard the news, I was shocked and didn't know what to do next. I stood in place and just looked around, disbelieving that all of the things I was experiencing were real and wishing that they were just a bad dream.

The military specialist that was manning the message center kept talking to me but I did not and could not hear him at that point. I just staggered over to a chair and sat down to try to comprehend the terrible news that I had just received. I just couldn't believe the call from Jay. I didn't want to believe it. I was stunned! I was pissed! I didn't know what I was, but I was not all there. The specialist called for an orderly and the orderly led me back to my room. The guys could sense that something was terribly wrong. The orderly spoke to a Staff Sergeant in whispered tones and the guys gathered around to lend me support. My thoughts were to just go back to sleep and hope that when I woke up, it would all be okay. It would be over and things would be back to normal. Like nothing had ever happened.

The next morning I was awakened by an Army Chaplain who explained to me what I could do and suggested options for me about the situation. He gave me information on travel plans that I could make and other travel tips I would need for a trip home.

He suggested that a train back to Michigan might be the best way for me to travel. Later in the day, a Supply Sergeant came by and fitted me with a new uniform to wear home. He asked one of the nurses to sew on my insignias. One of the fellows lent me a CIB, (Combat Infantry Badge) badge to wear. Aside from the unit insignias, it was the only metal I would ever wear. The Red Cross set me up with a travel companion, a very nice, pretty, young lady named Nancy.

The Army personnel department set me up with emergency leave papers and the next day I was on my way back to Detroit. The train ride from Chicago to Downtown Detroit took about seven hours total. Somehow I dozed off. It reminded me of the train ride from Detroit to Fort Knox; now nearly three years ago. I was no longer the young man I had been then. A lot of water had gone under the bridge since then. And, a lot of memories had come and gone, both good and bad.

We arrived in Detroit late that night and then took a cab to the old neighborhood. I was staying with my brother, Jay and his new wife Beth. Nancy had taken the taxi on to her family's place and told me she'd see me in a few days. It was great for me having family close by. My brother spent the night catching me up on all the happenings over the past two years. It seemed as if it was a lifetime ago, and in many respects it was.

The next morning, wearing some of my brother's clothes, I went to visit Sharon and Will's parents. Sharon and the baby were living with Will's parents. Billy was now just over a year old and was just beginning to walk around the furniture. He would never know his father.

We all got into small talk, avoiding the real reason we were all back together. Will's dad informed me that Will would be returning home in two days and the local mortuary was set to pick him up from the airport. There would be a Mass at St. Monica's, the local Catholic Church where they always attended and we would all travel to the cemetery together as a family. The day went both fast and slow. Fast because I felt like I was not a real participant. I was more of an observer. I felt as if I was watching it all through a fog.

The day of the actual funeral came and it was a day I had dreaded. We followed the hearse to the cemetery. For a winter day, it was not as cold as normal, but it was a clear blue sky, cool and crisp. I don't remember much, but I think I may have asked if I could be of any assistance and was politely refused.

The Navy had sent a Lt. Commander to help Sharon and Will's parents through the day. We were met at the cemetery by a Navy Honor Guard. They formed at the rear of the hearse and took Will's casket into the mausoleum, where the service was held. Throughout the day, I could not make up my mind if I was required to salute the Navy officers in attendance. The Navy LTC. must have noticed and finally told me that it was not required at funerals and other such functions.

I was at a loss as to whether I should be with the family or stay politely behind. That dilemma disappeared when Sharon took me by the arm so I could walk with the family. I sat with them as the ceremony took place. It was over in less than an hour. Sharon was presented with the burial flag and the next thing I knew, we were alone in the mausoleum to say our last goodbyes to Will. As we left the chapel area, I was met by my brother Jay and his wife Beth. She had taken charge of young Billy during the ceremony. He was fast asleep with his head resting on her shoulder.

We went back to Will's parent's house to have a bite to eat. The Navy officer came into the house with us and said his farewells. Beth, my sister June, and Sharon got things together as far as setting up the food was concerned, but no one was interested in eating or talking. After about an hour or so, Beth asked me if I needed to rest. She said I was looking pretty worn out. It seemed at that point that everyone agreed that I did need to get some rest. Before leaving, I gave Will's mom and dad a big hug and walked outside. A light snow had begun.

Later, we went back to my brother's house and I changed back into my "civvies" and laid down. I was totally exhausted and I had not done a thing. I woke up in the middle of the night and heard voices coming from the kitchen. I slipped on my pants and went out to see what was going on. To my surprise, it was nearly 7am in the morning. I must have slept nearly 18 hours. I guess I was totally exhausted. Nancy was in the kitchen and was already at the table having coffee with my brother and Beth.

Nancy explained to me that we would be returning to Great Lakes early the next morning. I told Nancy "I did not want to go back. I wanted to stay and help Will's family." Both Nancy and Beth chipped in that the best thing for me to do was go back, get healthy, and then worry about Will's family. The next morning Nancy and I boarded the train for the ride back to Chicago. I remember crying much of my waking hours while on the train. I was ashamed that I was crying like a baby. I just couldn't keep Will off my mind. I remembered the very first day we had met nearly 12 years before. I cried because I had lost my best friend and I cried because I lost my opportunity to play baseball. And I cried because I cried.

Chapter 8

SHARON'S STORY

From the moment I first laid my eyes on Will at St. Monica's Church, I knew I loved him. He was such a cutie, with brown hair that seemed as if it had a mind of its own, and he resisted all efforts to be tamed. Plus, he had a smile that would light up an entire room. When I first saw him, I could not tell how tall he was because he was sitting down, so I could only guess at how old he really was. He was sitting as much as a boy his age could sit. I watched during the mass to see if he would take Communion. That would give me a good idea of his age. Communion meant he was over 11 years old.

I had just turned 12 in April and had already had my confirmation, as most 11 and 12-year-olds did. "Good," I thought, he went to communion, which meant that he was not a sinner and he was at least 12. I didn't remember seeing him in school, so I wondered if maybe he was just a visitor to St. Monica's Church.

Just about then Karen whispered into my ear, "I see you looking at that boy. I wonder who he is?"

"Shh," I said. "Mom will hear you. But he is cute, isn't he?"

On the following Monday, I saw him again. There he was, in the office of our school; Harding elementary. Because I was the messenger for the fifth grade, I thought it would be okay for me to go to the office to see if my homeroom teacher had any messages that I needed to deliver.

"Good morning Sharon, What can I do for you?" the office clerk, Miss Truman asked me.

"Oh, I just stopped to see if there were any messages for Mrs. Noonan before I go to class."

"No. Sorry. No messages. Mrs. Noonan already stopped and picked them up. By the way, this young gentleman is Will. He is new to Harding and will be in Mr. Barr's class."

My heart sank. Will would be in the other class for sixth graders. I walked over and offered to shake Will's hand. He was very polite and said, "Hello, I am Will."

"And I am Sharon." I was hoping he didn't notice that I was blushing a little. With that brief introduction, I turned and left the office.

At lunch, I looked for Will, but he was sitting with a group of guys that included Jack, Bob, and Lou. Those three guys were inseparable. On the way to my table, I stopped for just a second so Will could see me and I nervously said; "Hello guys!" My heart was pounding. I thought he was just so cute. I later found out from one of the other girls that Will lived on Vaughn. Hmm, only a few blocks from me I thought.

Through that summer I would get my younger sister Karen or some of my girlfriends to walk by his house with me. I never once saw him and I began to wonder why he was never at home? Eventually, I found out that he spent a lot of time with Jack and the guys playing ball in the park. My mom did not allow me to go to the park, so I spent most of my time thinking of what it would be like to talk with him again. So I began to plan on how to get his attention and what I would say to him.

Finally, I got one of my friends that were in Will's class, to ask him if he could walk down Patton to school and help carry a science project. Will, being such a gentleman would help, I was sure. The following Monday, Will showed up as scheduled and with his friend Jack in tow. I asked my sister Karen to keep Jack busy so I could talk to Will. She said she would but in exchange, I had to make her bed for her for a week. So that was the deal that we made. To this day it may be the best deal I ever made.

That day, I did get to talk with Will and many other days throughout the remainder of the school year. And the debt to my sister continued to increase. But in the end, I'm not too sure that I really made her bed all the times that I had promised.

Throughout the summer it seemed that Will and Jack were always at the park playing baseball with the other guys. So, my best time to talk with Will was on Sundays after church. I always made sure to say "hello" to Will's parents too. They were very nice people and Will's mom and my mom would talk about cooking and taking care of the house.

One day, I heard Will's mom mention to my mom that she worked outside the home and it was hard to keep up the house and work full time too. She told my mom she was looking for some extra help and asked; "Do you know of anyone that I could hire?"

I jumped at the chance. "I could help out with your housework if you'd like."

My mom and Lois, (Will's mom) looked at me and said "Okay!" It was that easy! So I had a job and would be closer to Will.

In time, Lois became my mentor and a good friend. She taught me how to run the washing machine and make the beds. She was a stickler for details and wanted her home to be just right.

Whenever I could, I would linger in Will's room. He was a typical boy. He had a few toys from when he was younger, a model plane on his dresser and a box of baseball cards on his small desk.

After a few weeks, Lois asked me if I "liked Will?" I told her that I did, but that I hardly knew him. We were in different classes. She sat me down in the kitchen and said; "What I mean is do you like him more than just a fellow student?"

She caught me by surprise. I didn't know what to say, but I guess I must have blushed a lot because she just laughed and said to me; "Well it's okay to like him as more than just a friend. We all go through that." She then told me of how she and Bill, Will's dad, had met, dated and gotten married when he was home on leave from the war. It was a true love story with a very happy ending.

My favorite time at Harding was when the school dances started. Will was my boyfriend then and we would walk to school together every day. The nights of those dances were magical and Will and I would just dance together and have a great time. Will's best buddy, Jack, was kept busy for the most part by my sister Karen. She liked the idea that she could make Jack nervous. She also didn't mind that some of the other guys paid attention to her too.

When we were in high school we spent even more time together attending dances, dating and any other activities we could do together. Jack had bought an old car and fixed it up. We would double date at times if poor Jack could get a date. Every once in a while I would bribe Karen to go out with him just so Will and I did not have to be driven somewhere by his mom.

Jack was like a brother to Will and I. Sometimes at drive-in movies the two of them could replay a ball game that they had played together weeks ago. It became a joke that Will and Jack talked to each other on a date more than they did to the girls they were with. I thought it was pretty weird that Jack and Will could finish each other's sentences. Impressing girls was not on their agenda at that point.

We, like a lot of the teenagers in the Detroit area at that time, spent hours cruising Woodward Avenue. I gotta say, Jack's car's, (and he had a few), was always one of the nicer cars. If someone asked about his cars, he was quick to make a deal and sell them the car on the spot. But, he never made us walk home though.

One time, I remember there was a guy that asked if the car was for sale, and Jack told him "everything I have is for sale". He was just trying to be a smart ass. So the guy asked him about his girlfriend. Jack just laughed and told the guy, "You can't afford her." I think that was the last time that girl ever dated Jack.

After a while, I began to think of Will's mom as a second mother to me. I even fell into the habit of calling her "Mom". Lois always referred to me as "the daughter she never had." She had a little pet name for me; "Shar." And I loved it. I felt really comfortable around her. We could have some great conversations that my mom and I never had.

When I became a senior in high school, I began to work part-time at the tool and die shop that Will's parents owned. Will and Jack were not around much because they were always playing baseball somewhere. I was able to watch the guys play many times and it was pretty easy to tell that they had more talent than all the other guys on the team.

Will and Jack were starting to get a lot of attention from colleges and even some professional teams, to play ball. You could tell that Jack was not even thinking about college. He was anxious to go pro right from the start.

Will had a plan and was going to college to take aeronautical engineering. During our dates, that was one of his favorite topics. He wanted to be a pilot and fly jets. One of the larger colleges appealed to Will because the baseball coach had offered him a half ride scholarship which would allow Will to join the Navy ROTC program and take the flight training required.

Will left for college almost the same time Jack left for his rookie season as a professional ballplayer. It was getting pretty lonely in the neighborhood with them both gone. I began working full time at the shop and there I met Jack's older brother, Jay. When Jay got out of the military, he was looking for a career and Jack suggested he ask Bill for a job. He was a very nice guy who looked and acted a lot like Jack did and he fit right in with us.

Jay would stop by the office every so often and give me of a progress report on Jack and how he was doing with his baseball career. Everyone in the neighborhood was very proud of Jack, their hometown hero.

About that time we began to see that many of the other younger guys in the area were getting draft notices. The war in Vietnam was getting closer to home. When Will left for college, I began missing him terribly. For the past six years, we had hardly spent any time apart. I was not liking it but knew it was part of Will's plan to create a future for us. Sometimes we would talk about our future and the things we could do when we were married. I loved talking to Will about those things, it made me feel like an adult.

Lois noticed that I was moping around the shop one day and said to me, "You know, I miss him too. How would you like it if we planned a trip to go visit him some weekend?"

That lit me up. "Oh! I would love that! When do we leave?" Lois said; "Let's plan on a weekend, in about ten days."

Those ten days may have been the longest ten days of my life. We drove up to Will's school and watched him play a double hitter. Then we all had dinner together at a local restaurant. It was like old times again. I was so happy to be able to spend that time with him.

That night Will told me how lonely it was up there without me and he wished we could be together. He wanted me to transfer from the school I was attending and go to a local school so we could at least see each other more often. We finally came to a compromise; I would buy a used car and come to visit him when he was free from a weekend of ball games or his Naval training.

It was in his junior year at school that we made love for the very first time. To say the least, it was absolutely wonderful to be with him in that way. We were together many weekends after that until I discovered that I may be pregnant. I was scared and didn't know what to do. So I finally told Will and we visited a local doctor where he confirmed the pregnancy. I was afraid to tell my mom, so I did the next best thing and told Lois.

Lois was beside herself with joy. She gave me a little lecture but was smiling the whole time. Seeing that I was over 18, I did not need my parent's permission to get married, but Lois told me it would be the "right thing" to include my parents in the news and any plans that were going to be made.

We made plans for a small wedding in the town where Will went to school. My sister Karen was my "Maid of Honor" and Will's dad was his "Best Man." Later that night, I remember Will commented on the fact that he was missing his first ball game ever.

Our friend Jack was playing baseball when we got married. He sent us a nice gift of money that his brother Jay delivered with a message saying; "He was very sorry that he missed the wedding of his two best friends." I had the feeling that Jay and Beth had bought the card for Jack. We all knew how forgetful Jack could be and because he was more focused on playing baseball.

A few months later, I became a mother. We had a beautiful son. Will and I were so happy. We couldn't imagine ourselves as parents, but there we were. Our son looked just like Will. Same eyes and features, except he had dark hair like me. We named him "William Jack" after his dad and our best friend, Jack.

Soon after our son was born, Will left for flight training in Florida, and once again we were separated from each other. Will knew that as soon as he finished his training he was most likely going to Vietnam. I was so worried about his safety and prayed every day for his safe return. In the meantime, I was mostly focused on being the best mom I could to little Billy, which took up most of my days.

While Jack was gone, we received the bad news that he had been wounded in Vietnam. Jay brought a telegram into the shop that his family had received from the Department of the Army explaining that he was being sent to a hospital in Chicago. We were all in shock. We wanted to drop everything and go see him but we were told he was in very bad shape and still in a coma and may not make it through the transport home. This suddenly brought the reality of the Vietnam War too close to home.

Jay drove his mom and dad to Chicago to see Jack, but he had not regained consciousness during their visit. When Jay returned to the shop the following Monday, he was very down and filled us all in on Jack's status. The Army had sent him to the Great Lakes Hospital for a few reasons. For one, it was close to Detroit and family, plus it had the best head trauma unit available. More so than the local VA hospital that was closer to home in Allen Park, Michigan.

For nearly two weeks we got daily news from Jay which was mostly two words: No change. Then one morning Jay came in and told us that Jack was coming out of his coma, but the doctors still did not know the extent of his injuries yet. I wrote to Will and gave him the news. I had not told him yet of Jack's injuries because Will's dad, Bill told me to wait until we had some better news on Jack before we wrote to tell him about it.

Will always sent the same message home. "We flew another mission today and I am getting bored." Then he would give me a countdown as to how many days he had left on his tour. I missed him so much.

We were all elated the day that we received the phone call at the shop from Jack. It was so good to hear his voice, even though it was hardly above a whisper. We all told him to do what the doctors wanted him to do and that we would plan a trip over to see him very soon.

It was about two weeks later, as we were getting ready to leave for work one morning when a sedan from the Department of the Navy pulled up in front of the house. A Navy Lt. Commander (LTC) and a Navy Chaplain got out of the car and slowly walked up to the front door. I immediately had a sinking feeling in my stomach. I knew they had bad news.

Either Will was badly injured or he was dead. I prayed for the injury. Before they could ring the doorbell, I opened the front door and said; "Please come in."

The Chaplain introduced himself and the LTC and asked; "Are you Sharon Carter, the wife of LT. William Carter?"

"Yes, I am. Is Will still alive?"

"Mrs. Carter, would you like to sit down? Is there anyone in the house with you?"

"I live here with Will's parents and our son."

There was a lump forming in my throat and a sinking feeling in the pit of my stomach. Just as I finished speaking, Will's mom came in from the kitchen holding little Billy. Will's dad was coming down the stairs and hesitated when he saw the men. Then he continued down as we all gathered into the living room.

Before anyone could say a word, Bill proceeded over to the officers, shook hands and said. "Good morning I am Major William Carter, USMC retired. What can I do for you?"

The Chaplain asked all of us to please sit down and then relayed the message that Will had been killed while flying a "close air to ground support mission" in South Vietnam. Marine Corp. ground forces were able to go in and recover his remains. The Navy was 100% certain it was Will that had died in the crash. Along with his remains, the Marines had also recovered a few personal items that would be returned to us in the next few days.

The two officers stood up and told us they were very sorry for our loss. LTC Davis said he would accompany Will back and asked if there was a local funeral director we would like to have handle the funeral arrangements and burial? Bill looked in the local phone book and gave them the name and phone number of the Willis Funeral Home, just a few blocks from the house. They told us the Navy would take care of everything and would we like LTC Davis to assist us in planning Will's funeral? Bill thanked them for the offer but told them we would take care of the arrangements from here.

After the Naval officers left we all just looked at each other, stunned to know that our lives were now changed forever. Lois and I hugged each other and cried. Little Billy did not know what to make of the crying and the pacing that his grandpa was doing. Billy was a very happy child and had never seen his Mama, Papa, and Nana sad.

Bill picked up the phone and called the shop. He spoke a few words and hung up. A few minutes later the phone rang. Bill answered it and again spoke a few words to Jay. I could tell it was Jay, by some of the questions Bill had asked. "Was Jack able to travel? Could he get here within the next few days to attend Will's funeral?" Bill came over to the couch and sat with us and we all shed tears to lost futures, and wonderful memories of our most beloved Will.

Jay contacted Jack and the hospital at Great Lakes to determine if Jack was well enough to travel. The question was could Jack make the trip by car? Hospital personnel suggested that Jack could travel by train as long as he had someone travel with him. Jay contacted the Red Cross and arrangements were made for a travel companion for Jack.

When I finally had some time to be alone, I went through the personal items delivered to me by the Navy. Among the items were a few pictures of us all together when Billy was first born and the unopened letter I had sent to Will explaining that Jack had been injured in Vietnam.

When we saw Jack a few days later, I cried again. I cried because I was seeing him again and remembering all the great times we all had together as kids, knowing that our innocent lives were now changed forever. I also cried for Jack and the condition he was in. Aside from standing upright, he looked terrible. He was so skinny, gaunt and very pale. He had a very noticeable limp, was wearing a patch over his left eye and had bandages on his right hand.

We all hugged and did the small talk thing and then talked about how the service for Will was going to be. Jack seemed uneasy around the Naval Officers and at times he seemed as if he wanted to salute them, then wasn't sure. The ceremony and the burial went as well as could be expected. The Navy did a wonderful job in bringing us comfort. For their service, I will always be grateful.

Not knowing what the future would bring with the sudden loss of Will, I had to learn to trust that everything would be okay for Billy and I. It made me sad to think that Billy would never get to know how amazing his father was, but I was so very grateful Will had given me a son, that would always carry a part of him forever.

Chapter 9

JACK'S RECOVERY

Once I was back at Great Lakes I stopped being the model patient. I did not want to recover. I wanted my friend Will back. I wanted to play just one more ball game with him; even just one more inning. My progress did not go as quickly as anyone had wished. The eye patch came off and went on the other eye to tease the left eye to pick up some slack. It was something I didn't have to work very hard at. The eyes did what eyes would do.

The physical training went much slower and the docs had conflicting views. Should I exercise the leg muscles by walking more, or with more motion? I did my best to avoid any type of therapy. It was just too much work. I became an old timer at Great Lakes. My head injuries seemed to be a thing of the past but I did have some difficulty in remembering certain things from my past and things that were told to me, like doctor's appointments. To compensate, I began to carry a small notebook with me to write things down. The one thing I wanted to forget, that I could not forget was Will's death.

The Chicago Cubs sent over a representative to discuss my progress and to see if I would be available for spring training. The doctors at Great Lakes talked to the doctors from the Cubs and it was determined that I would probably benefit from a change of scenery and have something else for me to get focused on. Although the Navy doctors did not believe I was ready for such increased physical activity, I also could see the doubt in the eyes of the Cubs doctors although they were tight-lipped. I often wondered if the Cubs were acting out of pity.

It was just a few more weeks until spring training and nearly four months until the end of my enlistment. I was nearing my 24th birthday. Not old, but getting near the age that my age would make a difference to the ball club.

There was also another small item that had to be overcome. I was still an official member of the US Army. So, I went to see the Army personnel officer to review my options. The army had extended my enlistment during my stay at Great Lakes so my hospital benefits and therapy would continue to be covered. One thing I found humorous was that I continued to be paid by the Army and received another promotion to Staff Sgt. while I was at Great Lakes.

The Army Personnel Officer thought it would be best for me not to take my discharge just yet. He suggested that seeing I was not physically ready to resume my baseball career and that I should continue therapy, maybe somewhere closer to home or at Fort Knox. The Army had a few jobs I could handle that were non-combative roles such as Mess Sergeant or even as a Training Sgt. Either way, I would have to postpone my discharge.

After some deliberation, I finally decided to accept my discharge and was granted leave until my enlistment was up in September. At that point, I arranged to attend spring training with the Cubs and also do some rehab work at the local VA Hospital.

My younger brother Jody had just graduated from high school and was looking for something to do, so I hired him as my personal assistant. Aside from the money I had put away when I was working on cars before my enlistment, I had also saved some of my salary that I earned during my year and a half of playing baseball. In addition, I had accrued money while I was in Vietnam and my military pay that I had accrued while at Great Lakes. So, I was not entirely without funds at that point and if I watched my pennies I was probably okay for a year or so. The Cubs had taken out an insurance policy when they first signed me to guard against loss of investment they had made in me as a player. The Cubs had agreed to pay me a small salary during Spring Training.

It was strange walking onto a ball field again after all the time I had spent away from baseball and instead spent in a war zone or in the hospital at Great Lakes. Then I realized it has been less than three years since I last played ball. So much had happened in those three years.

The Cubs assigned me to train with a group of players that were coming off injuries suffered over the past season. There were a collection of assorted injuries, mostly from bad arms and broken bones that had not healed.

When I first arrived at the facility I went into the minor league clubhouse to see what type of equipment I could scare up. Aside from military uniforms, I no longer owned a ball glove or spikes, or for that matter civilian clothes. The Army doctors and therapist had suggested that I avoid wearing spikes until my balance returned. I was still using my cane, but I had put it aside a week ago to try to force myself into regaining my footing and hopefully make my injuries less noticeable.

The first day went well. One of the minor league infielders gave me an extra glove he had acquired during winter ball and the clubhouse manager gave me a set of old spikes that had been tossed away from one of the major league players. (Note: all good clubhouse managers salvaged a lot of items that were tossed away by the players. They saved them for some of the lower minor league players or to donate to the local recreation teams). Although the doctors had said not to wear the spikes I did put them on and then quickly took them off. My feet and legs were certainly not ready for spikes.

After I suited up, I located the assigned field and picked up a partner, who like me, was recovering from injury. Ray had been at Single-A ball when I had passed through back when I first started with my pro career. The assistant trainer came over to the field, introduced himself to the players and took notes on the type of injuries and the age of the injuries. I did note that I was the second youngest player in the rehab field. Ray was the youngest by just less than two weeks.

In the afternoons, I would spend my time at the VA hospital in therapy. After about a week or so, the club allowed me into the batting cages to determine how much I had lost with the batting eye. I was surprised to see that I was no longer able to determine if the ball coming at me was a breaking pitch of a fastball. My reaction time to the ball was way out of whack too. I was guessing more than I was reacting to the pitch.

On my next turn in the cage, about a week later, I was standing around when someone hit a low line drive toward the group of guys I was with. All the guys were able to get out of the way, but I could not. The ball hopped up and hit me in the right thigh. I guess I was lucky it was not my bad left leg. The trainer came over to check me out and made a comment on my reaction time.

A few days later the general manager for minor league player development invited me into his office and gently told me that the club was concerned that I could get injured while being on the field. The club was suggesting that I stay on the sidelines and restricted my activities to play catch until I could react to the action going on around me.

After another week, as the players on the injury list began to either be cut by the club or assigned to minor league camps, the GM called me into his office and told me the club was cutting me. He explained that I was too injured to be able to do anything baseball-wise this season. He shook my hand and told me the club would be more than happy to have me back when I caught my breath and could return to normal baseball activities.

My brother Jody arrived from Michigan a few days later, after graduating from high school. I took a taxi to the airport to pick him up and the first thing he said to me was; "What no wheels of your own?"

Once we got him settled we went looking for a car. Although Jody was only a few years younger than I, he seemed decades younger. He had missed the draft because he had a deformed small toe. He was classified 4-A. The deal Jody and I struck were that he would help me with general things and I would provide him with room and board. He planned to attend college so the deal would work for both of us. The VA declared me to be 80% disabled, and I was now receiving my benefits, so for a while, not having a job was less of a problem.

My brother Jody also delivered a message to me from Will's dad, Bill. He had talked with Lois about the accounts that I had back in Michigan with his company and was a bit surprised at the amount I had saved up over the years. He asked that I call him at the shop when I could.

It took Jody and I a few days to get into sync with each other, but we finally did. Jody was a little shorter than I but carried more weight. He was also strong as a bull. I began to rely on him as my workout partner and it was working well for both of us. He would attend my PT sessions at the VA, talk to the instructors and set up my workout routines.

Somehow I picked up a magazine that had peaked my attention as I wait for the PT instructor at a session. The article dealt with a treasure hunt up in Canada on Oak Island. For the most part, I thought the article was pure bullshit, but there was a nagging something I could not let go of. As it were, the article got me thinking about the other things I had been missing in life, but, I soon forgot the magazine and the article and remembered I had to call Bill in Michigan.

A few days later Bill and I finally got together by telephone after I had missed him a few times. After asking about my health and rehab, he told me I had to get a phone. Frankly, I had never ever thought about getting a phone. I promised Bill that I would. He bragged about little Billy and got me caught up with all the local news. He told me my brother Jay was now in charge of one area of the plant and they were talking about expanding. He asked if I wanted to come back to Michigan and he would put me to work. I softly told him I was still following the baseball dream but I truly appreciated the offer.

He then stunned me by telling me how much money I had accumulated over the years and that I should consider investing some of the money for my future. I asked if he had any suggestions. Bill got very quiet and asked if I would be interested in investing in the plant's expansion? We talked around the idea for a few minutes and he suggested that he would send the paperwork to a firm that would look things over and offer advice. I agreed to think about it. He told me that everyone missed me and were pulling for me. Then he asked when I was coming home for a visit?

Bill laughingly told me that my brother's young daughter was walking now and following little Billy around every time they were together. He told me it reminded him of Sharon when she would walk by the house looking for Will. I said I would get back to him when I could. I hung up the phone and cried like a baby. Was I so self-absorbed that I had forgotten my best friend?

Soon, I got interested in reading for something to do. At first, I followed up on the treasure article I had come across before. Then I looked into other treasure hunts. The seas around Florida were full of sunken treasure ships and I thought maybe I would become a treasure hunter if the baseball thing did not work out. One good thing was the reading got me to think about other things than my problems.

Jody and I would discuss his assignments from school and many of them were very interesting. Once in a while, I would attend one of his classes with him. They weren't too bad, but it seemed that the kids were awfully young. It was also surprising to me on how they dressed acted and talked. Jody seemed to fit right in with them and was a different person at school than he was at home.

Soon after, I started jogging a little and was surprised at how tired I got. My leg would ache for days at a time after even a short jog. I made regular visits to the Cubs minor league facilities and could get up a game of catch with one of the guys. It was great being on the field again. The arm was fine.

The legs were gaining strength, but the eye was still a problem. Even in games of soft toss, I had difficulty judging the ball's arrival to the glove. Playing pepper with the guys was the best for me. My eyes began to adjust to the speed and motion of the ball. I tried glasses with different lenses on each side. They were of some help, but not entirely the answer.

Jody came home one day from class and told me he had seen the college ball team practicing and had stopped to watch. Jody said they were terrible. Worse than when he had been in high school. He told me I should stop by sometime and get a good laugh.

On most days, Jody had the car and I was on my own. I began taking walks to strengthen my legs and to see what else was happening around the neighborhood. I would plan my walks to increase the distance and still make it home without having to stop and rest. Although we were out in the boonies, many of the folks in our area began to be accustomed to my walks. From time to time, they would stop and chat for a few minutes. All in all, I had some very nice neighbors.

In late September, the minor league baseball season was over and the town began to slow down. About that time, I received a letter from the Cubs saying they were terminating our relationship. I was heartbroken and vowed to prove them wrong.

Years later as I reflected on the situation, I knew that they had made the decision based on what was best for the Cubs organization. I had begun to realize that organizations could not carry people who could not produce for the organization.

Winter spent in a summer town is really boring. My walks got boring as some of the businesses closed for the winter and there were less people on the roads. I began reading again, this time history books, and novels that had a historical bend. I also read many articles on the war in Vietnam. For the most part, the articles were pure BS. The folks writing the articles skipped over many of the good things we had done while being there. The articles did not tell about the hospital, schools, and tools to farmers that helped the Vietnamese to live better lives. They totally skipped over the fact that the North Vietnamese were brutal to their own citizens.

After a while, I stopped reading the articles. Jody decided to take a trip to Michigan and I agreed to go along. It had been nearly two years since I had seen anyone from home in that time period. We planned our trip for Thanksgiving, taking a few days before, and a few days after.

As we were packing, I was reminiscing as to the times Will and I had spent Thanksgiving trying to out-eat each other. I remembered his mom saying we were eating ourselves sick and would regret it. She laughed all the while at "her boys" as she said they had become gluttons. I remembered how she referred to us as "her boys." A small thing at the time, but it was a big deal now. I wondered if I was still considered "her boy?"

We got home to Detroit Metro Airport just as a winter storm was going to hit. The weatherman had predicted four inches of snow. Welcome to Michigan! The airport was filled with G.I.'s coming and going. Families saying goodbye and greeting their loved ones returning home. The guys in uniform looked so young. Much younger than I had been nearly four years ago. Funny as it seemed, I thought I recognized all of them as guys I had served with. Except for the guys in the airport were so young.

Other travelers looked at the G.I.'s with different looks than I had seen when I shipped out. You could spot some of the G.I.'s not wearing uniforms and I had to believe it had to do with the ongoing war in Vietnam. I did not witness the changing of the attitudes of the folks at home. It drew me back to my departure more than four years ago. A lifetime ago. Many lifetimes ago.

Bill met us at the airport with my brother Jay. They both looked great! Jay had put on a few pounds, but Bill looked the same as he had years ago. As we approached the neighborhood on that cold, snowy night, my thoughts came rushing back of the days when we had snowball fights and built snow forts. I remembered so well how much Will and I would stand off the remainder of the guys and sometimes win.

Bill and Jay dropped Jody and I off at my childhood home and told us that they would be back tomorrow to pick us up. Mom looked great! Not much different than when I last saw her nearly two years ago. Dad looked worse. He was coughing, wheezing and generally not doing good. We gave great big hugs all around and mom said that Jody and I would share the downstairs bunk-bed room. I laughed and said; "But Ma! Jody snores!"

Mom told me she had been saving up some mail that I had received while I was living away. I was surprised because I could not imagine who would be sending mail to an address I hadn't used in nearly six years. I told her to let me have it and I'll go through it when I got time. Jody begged off and said he had friends he wanted to go visit and hit the door running. I figured it must be a girl. I sat in my old bedroom from six years ago. It was an odd feeling, being here again. Everything was so different, and yet, so much the same.

There was a small box addressed to me as S. Sgt. I hadn't thought one second about my days in the Army since I had left Florida to come home. I opened the box and it was a collection of military medals. I recognized the Combat Infantry Badge, but the rest was kind of a mystery. I came out of the room and sat at the table with my dad. I asked him if he could identify any of the medals?

He picked up a few and you could see his eyes gloss over, going back to when he had been a young soldier fighting for his life in Germany. He asked; "is there a letter with these medals?"

"Oh, I forgot to look."

I pulled a folded sheet of paper out of the bottom of the box. Pretty much a form letter that explained I had earned these medals during my service in the United States Army. They listed each medal and the description of each of them. One each: Silver Star. one each, Purple Heart, one each, Vietnam Service Medal, one each, American Defense Medal, one each, Expert Marksman Badge: Rifle, Pistol, and a few others.

As I looked over to ask my dad a question, he was weeping and sobbing behind his hands. I halted and waited a few minutes until he was ready and asked him about the medals and what they meant. He took a few minutes and then told me of the general meaning and status of the various medals.

He then said to me, "Son you are a hero in anybody's book."

"Dad," I said, "the true heroes never made it home."

That night, I didn't sleep much between a strange bed, too many memories, and finding those medals. I know I did sleep some because visions of the night in Vietnam came back. This time I was watching the battle from a different viewpoint. The images were mixed together. Some in the jungle, some during that nighttime firefight, and then a few of the three-day pass I had during my tour. It was all very weird.

Later, I heard Jody come into the room and hopped up onto the top bunk. As soon as he hit the rack he was sleeping and started snoring away. Ah, the joys of youth!

In the morning, Jay showed up with Beth and the kids. Gosh, it was noisy. Much the same as when I was a kid making all the noise. Then my sister June showed up with her husband Ray and their two little boys, Raymond and Robbie. Needless to say, they added to the noise. So, I got into the car for the short ride to the Carter's house. Mom had promised to bring dad and the kids over to the Carter's for dinner. Jody just continued to snore away through it all.

Oh, the memories started coming back in a flood. Delivering newspapers, shoveling walks, all the things that Will and I had done as kids.

I didn't know it would be this hard. The last time I had been here, was at Will's funeral. At that time I had not been in full control. The meds had dulled my senses and the grief had been overwhelming.

As I entered the Carter's house, I was filled with mixed memories of Will and me at the dinner table eating supper. Memories of the previous visit for the funeral. Memories, memories and more memories.

Sharon came over and gave me a tremendous hug, followed by Lois and then Bill. There was a little boy there and for a second it did not dawn on me as to who he was. Then it hit me. It was Billy Jack Carter. I said his name in my head. Then I stopped and said it over and over in my head, Billy Jack, Billy Jack. It sounded like he was a country singer.

The little guy came over, put out his hand to shake and said, "My name is Billy. I was named for my Daddy and my Grandpa." I shook his hand and said "I am Jack. I am a friend of your Mom and Dad and your Grandma and Grandpa."

"My mom said I could hug you."

"I would like that."

He looked like his daddy as I remembered him, but a smaller version. As we hugged, my love for my brother Will spilled out and I cried like a baby. I did not want to let go. I wanted to be with Will again. To do the things we once did.

After a few moments, I felt a hand on my shoulder, it was Sharon and she too was crying. I stood and gave her a hug and all I could say is; "I'm sorry, I am so sorry."

She looked at me and said; "there is nothing you need to be sorry for. We are all just thankful that we still have you."

Later my family showed up and we all ate a great Thanksgiving dinner. We told stories about how good the "good old days" were and some of the stunts we had pulled as kids. Later that evening I went back to Jay's house to stay overnight. He then drove Jody and me back to the airport a few days later.

Jay sat me down and said; "Dad showed me your medals. That's quite a collection you got there. You must have gone outside the wire huh?" He then slapped me on the back, gave me his Jay laugh and went to bed.

The following morning Jay gave me a rundown on how the plant was doing. He told me the plant and expansion was doing very well and we were all making great money. He also added that Bill was thinking of buying out another fellow who was retiring and looking to sell. He asked me what I was doing with my money. I told him I was reinvesting it back into stocks and things that Bill had suggested.

"To tell the truth," I said, "I had no idea how much money was there."

"Damn," my brother said. Then he just laughed, leaned over and hit me on the shoulder.

Chapter 10

EDUCATING THE UNEDUCATED

The new semester at the college was beginning at that time and I had been kicking around signing up for a class or two. I was interested in how folks possessed the ability to write stories. And more importantly, how did they come up with the ideas on what write about. The VA had a program for Vets to help pay for some schooling, so I thought I might as well take the money while the taking was good.

After listening to my brother Jody, I signed up for a basic English class. It was a required class for any degree, so to me, it was like killing two birds with one stone. Jody had told me that most of the class was reading books and writing reports. Read, I could. Writing reports? Well, we'll see. At that time my only hope was that we would be assigned the subject matter and would not be required to think up our own storylines.

On my first day of class, I was in for a rude awaking and unpleasantness. The English instructor may have been younger than I was. He had long hair, dressed in what I would consider rags and needed a good shave. My fellow classmates, kids really, were all much younger than I. And they were rude. In addition to being rude, my fellow classmates did not want to do their assignments.

They did, however, have more than enough to say about current events and the ongoing war in Vietnam. I did get into quite a few discussions with them about the principles of the war. Being a Vet and somewhat older, I was able to hold my own. I did learn that when they were losing an argument they had a tendency to raise their voice. It was then I was aware that I had once learned it was better to raise your argument and not your voice.

There were many times when I just shook my head in disbelief. How could these young folks get so opinionated and still not be able to vote? Iron Mike had once told me that "when you raise your voice people stopped hearing you."

The bookstore had not gotten the textbook that was required for the class, so the first couple of classes were a bit boring for me to say the least. The instructor filled most of the class time reviewing the reason we were in the class and handing out short assignments to write in class in order to determine our current levels of abilities.

In those first few classes, I just sat back to try to see where the thought process of the class was. To me, it was a mixed bag. I could see that some of the students were here for the same reason that I was. It was a class needed towards a degree. Others were here seeking knowledge not found between the covers of a book.

The textbooks and other materials that we were used were not much use to me. They were required and that pretty much said it all, I read them, did the assigned summaries and reports, and that was pretty much it. Near the end of the semester, one of the fellows asked the instructor if he had an opinion on the war in Vietnam. That started an interesting conversation The class seemed to be split on the support and on the validity of the war. Needless to say, I fell into the camp that was solidly behind our troops serving in Vietnam.

One evening in January, as I was crossing through a campus building on my way to my car, I heard the unmistakable sound of a baseball hitting a mitt. Someone was playing catch in the building. I walked toward the sound and ended up in the entrance of a gym.

There was a small group of guys playing catch and talking about how good it was to be back at it. I noticed an older guy standing near one corner. He was watching the fellows closely and at times offered some tips. I figured he must be the coach.

Then it struck me, the coach was wearing his ball cap just like every Marine I had seen wearing their "cover." (Military personnel does not wear hats, they wear covers.)

One of the fellows missed a ball and it rolled to my feet. The fellow yelled out, "A little help?" So leaned down, picked up the ball and tossed it back.

The coach then hollered at me, "Hey fellow this is a closed practice, for team players only." That did not phase me in the least. I walked into the room, approached the coach and said to him, "Gunny, I am just a broken down old ballplayer." (Note: a Gunnery Sergeant in the Marine Corp. is a special rank achieved when a Marine proves to be proficient in all aspects of weapons and Marine Corp. traditions. The rank is equal to that of an Army SFC, (Sergeant First Class in the Army, E-7)

"What makes you think I am a Marine?"

"Gunny, I can see it in the way you wear your ball cap and your stance when talking."

"All of you says 'Marine'."

"Well, you are right, I was. I am a Marine but never got to Gunny. You military?"

"I was. I've been discharged about two years ago. Army Sgt."

"You on the faculty here?"

"Nope, I am a student. Just started this fall."

"What are you doing in here?"

"I heard the guys tossing the ball around and got curious."

"You play any ball?"

"I was playing Triple-A until I got drafted."

"Not playing now?"

"No, I was wounded in Vietnam and I am still recovering."

"Yeah, I was over there too. It was a real mess from what I remembered. You have any problems fitting in with the students on campus?"

"No problems except many of them are still wet behind the ears. And lack of true life experiences to form a truthful point of view. I suspect many of them are just repeating things they hear."

."So are you down here for spring training next month?"

"I'm not sure yet. I got put on medical leave. It was non-baseball related, by the Cubs organization because of my war injuries and I do not have a club to go to now."

"So what is your plan to get back into the game?"

"I am not sure yet."

"Well, why not work out with us and see what happens?"

"Well Marine, that sounds great! Thank you."

"They call me Coach Duane."

"Okay Coach see you tomorrow. What time should I be here?"

"Be here about 6 pm. What's your name soldier?"

"Jack!

Jack. I'm Duane."

As we shook hands, he said; "Please call me Duane or Coach. I just got this job myself, so we'll learn together."

The next evening Coach Duane met me at the door at the gym and told me he had met with the Athlete Director and because I had been a professional ballplayer, I could not work out with the team. But, I could work out as an unpaid "Assistant Coach." He asked if I would I be okay with that?

"Sure!" I said. "That would be great!"

Coach Duane then called the team together and introduced me to the team as "Coach Jack." I actually had official duties. I did station coachings such as infield drills, outfield drills, and hitting instructor. As the players went through the drills, so did I. I could feel myself getting stronger and quicker with the glove. I did, however, have problems seeing a pitch and reacting to the pitch, and I could not do much running above a slow jog.

As funny as it seemed, I did not agonize over the fact that I was having problems hitting. A few of the young guys were having more problems than I was. For the guys having hitting problems, I taught them good bunting skills. It all came back to me as to what I had been taught years ago.

Chapter 11

THE COMEBACK KID

Near the middle of February, I went over to the Cubs training facility and asked to see the head trainer. It was the same trainer I had met the year before. I asked him to give me an evaluation as to my physical ability to workout with the minor league team. I felt I was ready and had made loads of progress working out with the college team. I was still disappointed that I could not run at full speed, but I felt I would still progress some more in the future.

The Trainer checked with the front office and got the Okay. I was told to be ready the next morning at 7:30am, prior to team workouts.

Going through the workouts went fine and they said I could work out on a ten-day contract with the low minor leaguers and injured players. I was told; "Be back the next day at 8am."

So, my long trek back into baseball began early the next morning. It was like being back in the rookie ball, seven years ago. What seemed like a lifetime ago. Many lifetimes ago.

The arm came back first. Within a few days, I was throwing better than anyone else in the camp. The batting cage was another story. I still could not determine the rotation or spin on the ball. I could not track the ball onto the bat. My hand-eye coordination was off too.

The team was generous enough to send me to the team eye doctor to be evaluated for glasses. The glasses helped slightly, but not to the degree I needed to be a professional hitter. On reflection, I had been a natural hitter in my younger days and had often wondered how others could not see and react to hit the ball like I did. It came back to me about the days Will and I had played together and he went through the development as a hitter. Will had learned to use the skills God gave him and worked hard to improve. I no longer had the sharpness of those skills.

The Cubs extended my contract week to week. They explained it was necessary for insurance reasons. I was okay with that. I still had a chance.

After about two weeks into it, the pitching coach came over to me. Pulled me out of the infield drills and asked if I had ever thought of pitching?

The Trainer told me that my arm strength was better than most pitchers the Cubs had in camp and it may be my shot back into baseball. To me it was all I needed to hear, I was game to try anything at that point.

I told him I had pitched some in high school and that I had been okay. More like a power pitcher.

He laughed and said; "We see a lot of young ones like that here." He asked that I stick around for the pitcher/catcher camp after lunch. My heart was soaring. It was difficult to keep my excitement in check.

Later that day at the camp, they had me pitch batting practice to the squad. They told me it was to get me used to being on the mound again and to work on my form.

After throwing on and off for about 15 minutes, they shut me down and told me to come back the next day. Again, nervous like before. I was learning something new. A new position for me.

After a few days, the coaches added baseball grip techniques to the drills and began to teach me grips to throw breaking pitches. The arm was great, but the left leg began to give me problems. The calf muscle that had been rebuilt at Great Lakes was not keeping the pace with the strength required to do what I was asking it to do.

The club gave me a few days to recover and took the opportunity to visit the VA and have the doctors look at the leg. It was not good news. They told me the leg was about as strong as it was going to be and at that point, I was better than they had expected me to be. They added that the leg would strengthen with time but it would never be normal. I knew that normal was not good enough and unless there was a minor miracle in my future, I may not be playing ball.

In the spring, I went back to training and discussed the findings with the Cubs. They told me to stay in camp and work day today.

The pitching coach said: "After all, pitchers don't pitch every day, but the legs are important because they form the foundation. No foundation or a weak foundation is not good."

Another week went by. A day on the mound and a day off. But, the leg just got weaker. I kind of knew then that it was over for me.

Once again, I went to the Director of Minor League Player Development. I thanked him for all the Cubs had done for me, and for the opportunity to try to restart my career. He told me they were sorry that it did not work out and that if a position I could handle came up, they'd give me a call. My dream had ended with a pat on the back and a sincere handshake from the Cubs.

When I was heading home, I thought about the dreams I'd had since I was a young guy with Will and I playing ball. All the good times. But after all the years of following my dream, it was now over.

I missed a few classes and did not return to coach the ball team. I needed time to mentally heal. The memories and dreams came back. The tears too. Plenty of tears. Tears for a lost dream. Tears for my lost friend. My Brother. My Will.

A few days later, in the early evening, I heard a knock on the door. "Who in the hell is that?" I wondered. "No one has ever visited me before."

Jody had a new girlfriend and was spending more and more time over at her place, so I knew it was not him. I went to the door and there stood Coach Duane. When I answered the door the first thing he said to me was; "Soldier you look like shit. What's going on and where have you been?"

"Coach, I got cut."

"So, that means you didn't need to shave, take a shower, brush your teeth?"

"Sorry coach, I guess I just lost track of time."

"Well, I came over to take you to dinner, to find out what's going on and generally to catch up."

"I don't think I can handle that tonight"
"Remember this, you are not the first G.I. to have their dream cut short. It is the price that is paid by us so our families can live free.

Didn't you tell me your dad was a Vet? Didn't you tell me that your brother was a Marine? Did they come home and whine about the raw deal they got? Did either your dad or your brother tell you how pissed they were to have protected their country? How much they had missed in life? Jack, get your head out of your ass and get on with life."

"Well coach, my leg gave out. It was not, and never will be strong enough to play pro ball."

"Okay So what's your plan?"

"Coach, I don't know. I haven't given it any thought"

"Well think about this. I can still use you to help with the team. So if you want to stay in the game, come on back."

"Okay. How's the team doing?"

"Not too bad, but they miss you. They don't know they do. But they do."

"Okay. When do you want me back?"

"Be back tomorrow morning at 9am. And oh, take a shower. Okay?"

The next morning I returned to coaching. Maybe I had found something to do with my life after all.

Later in the week, the Athletic Director and I sat down and worked out an agreement as a Contract Employee of the Athletic Department. I would not be part of the faculty, but a general contract employee whose duties would be outlined by the baseball coach, Duane Harris. The position came with a small salary. Just enough to pay my rent and gas for the car that Jody always drove.

As the school year ended, Jody and I planned a visit to Michigan prior to the new semester. Part of my service contract was that I had to continue perusing my degree. So I began to double up on my classes and to my surprise, I did fairly well. Although my views did not always agree with the professors and my fellow students. I began to notice that Jody and I would no longer refer to Michigan as being home. We were now Floridians.

Jody had decided to take his girlfriend Carol, with us back to Michigan to meet the folks. He told me she was pushing him toward marriage so he thought that meeting the clan may chase her off. We flew back to Michigan and once again Jay picked us up at the airport.

On the way, Jay brought up the subject of lending mom and dad a few bucks so they could get out of the Projects. So the three of us hatched a plan to lend them the money to purchase a home. We stayed at Jay's for the trip and enjoyed his growing family. His daughter was now a little lady, and thank God she looked more like her mom. His son, Junior was in kindergarten. The baby, Judy was a real charmer and just beginning to jabber a lot and walk around the furniture.

The following day we went to visit Bill, Lois, Sharon, and Billy. Bill was not looking well, but his limp was now more pronounced and he looked much thinner than when I had last seen him. Lois looked great, a few more lines around the eyes, but just great. Sharon looked better than ever. She was now a woman. She had added a few pounds but they looked great on her. I gave her a big hug and I could hardly let go.

Billy was something else. Very tall for his age. He was nearly 8 years old, and as tall as Will had been when we first met nearly 15 years ago. I attempted to give him a hug, but he would not have it. He did shake my hand though. Said hello, and asked to be excused, and went outside.

We sat around and discussed the past years we had been apart and the general condition of the businesses, that we jointly owned.

Bill told me that he had been investing some of my profit sharing into different stocks. He believed that automatic machines and computers would be money makers in the future. I asked if I had enough ready cash to give some to my parents. Bill laughed and said; "Yeah, no problem there."

Sharon had finished college with a degree in finance and was now the Comptroller of the companies, as they expanded. We set up a time to meet on the following Monday to get a bank account started in my name.

That following Monday, Sharon and I went to the bank to open the account. The following day, my parents, my brothers and I all met at the real estate company and paid the money required. My parents were now homeowners for the first time in their lives.

A few weeks later, Jody, Carol and I returned to Florida and during the trip, I discussed that maybe we should buy a house down there and stop paying rent. Carol volunteered to do some house hunting and would give us a report within a few days. Jody looked over at me and rolled his eyes.

Evidently meeting the clan did not dissuade her from marrying my brother. In fact, it seemed as if the clan had convinced her that Jody and I needed her or we would never wash or eat correctly. So, much for Jody's Master Plan. He was now even closer to being married than he was when we had left for Michigan.

The Christmas season was now upon us and Jody had come to the decision that maybe, just maybe, married life would not be so bad. He had recently graduated from college and was actively looking for a full-time job. Carol was still looking for a house best suited for our needs.

Just after the new year began, Carol finally found a great house for us. It was a home where an elderly couple had moved into a condo so they would not have to care for all the property.

The property was a ways outside of the city and somewhat remote. And it came with a small orange grove which made Jody decide he wanted to become a farmer.

"Good luck with that," I told him. I liked the property because it offered enough space for when we had visitors from Michigan. I was now thinking of having others share my good fortune.

Finally, Spring came and the baseball season was starting. Again, I signed on as a Coach and was getting into a groove with the team and methods of teaching baseball to the players.

It's easy to just pass through life and never stop to smell the roses. I guess I did that pretty well as the years passed. Then one day that whole rose bush, roots, thorns, and flowers hit me square in the face. I got a call from Sharon. She was worried about both Bill and Billy. She asked if I could come home for a quick visit?

Chapter 12

YOUNG BILLY

School sucks. The teachers are total assholes and the kids are all geeks. My mom is spending too much time at the plant and on the road developing new business contacts. I love my mom and my grandparents, but I hate the fact I never can go anywhere. The other kids go on vacations. One kid has been to Disney World three times.

Hell, I haven't even been outside of Michigan three times. My mom is now on my ass for drinking a beer with my buddies. She doesn't realize that I am 14 years old and no longer a baby. I am even shaving now and get looks from the woman if I miss a few days. I even got sent home from school one day and told to shave before I came back.

Plus, I get tired of her telling me how my dad was such a perfect person. He's dead! He was dead before I ever had a chance to meet him. Damn! I just wish he were here now. As a guy, I am sure he would straighten my mom out. My mom would drop me at school on most days and would try to talk to me. I hated those rides to school. Most of the talks she gave me every time was all just BS!

One day she told me my Uncle Jack was coming for a visit and would spend a few days getting reacquainted with us and spend some time with his own family. I knew he was not my true uncle but was my dad's best friend when they were my age. He was the Uncle of my best friend Nicole, whose dad was "Uncle Jack's" brother, Jay.

Mom said he would be here Saturday, "So don't make any plans."

So, on Saturday he showed up. He looked like a much older version of the guy in the pictures with my mom and dad. I slightly remember him from the few times he had been here before for visits. Grandma and Grandpa treated him like a son. I had heard that he was like a son to them, and now I could see it first hand. It kinda made me wonder where I fit in. My dad had been and always would be number one to Grandma and Grandpa.

One thing that did impress me was he was a college baseball coach. If there was one thing in my life I loved, it was baseball. My high school coach told me I was an average ballplayer although he often said I could do much better. But, he always said, "you'd need to work a lot harder than you do." I liked baseball, but I also had other things I liked to do like working on old cars. I couldn't wait to take drivers training.

Coach Jack asked me about school and if I was active in other things. I told him school was OK, when, actually I was not doing well in school. Sometimes my classes were a real drag.

I told him I had a ball game later in the day and asked if he would like to watch. He said "sure, I'd like to see if you measure up."

I was thinking, "What in hell does that mean? Measure up? Measure up to what?" I let it slide. Sometimes the old folks did not know what they were talking about.

Mom drove us over to the ball field. Only a few of the guys were there. So, I hopped out and walked ahead of the "old folks". I saw my "Uncle" walk over and have a brief conversation with the Coach.

Later on, I learned that Jack had told the Coach he was also a Coach. A college coach from Florida. Jack told me that by being a coach in college, he was obligated to tell my coach that he was NOT scouting players, but watching a game for fun.

My coach had me playing first base. Not much of a challenge for me. As the game was going on, my mom, like all mothers, cheered and groaned. Jack was like a statue, no emotions at all.

Later, I asked Jack what he thought of the team and the game. He told me he thought some of the players were not bad, and some were probably playing in a league where they would top out and not progress any further. He said there were a few lazy players; players that he thought could do much better but were too lazy to work at it.

So I asked him, "Who's the best player?"

He told me "The shortstop. He may be able to play in college and maybe even the lower pros if he progressed a little more."

Then I asked him; "Where am I on your list?"

He told me with no emotion; "You may be the laziest player on the team. You have all the tools. Good hand-eye coordination, size, strength, and some foot speed, and your arm is pretty good too."

"You got all of that by watching one game?"

"Yup and many games just like it over the years."

"Will," he said, "when that low liner was hit toward first, you didn't even make a stab at it."

"Two things JACK! I am BILLY, NOT WILL! Will was my dad and he is dead! And why should I dive for a ball I cannot play?"

"You need to make the effort because you and your teammates need a leader. Someone needs to step up and lead the team."

"Well excuse me for living!"

After that, everyone was quiet on the way home. I could tell my mom was a little sad that Uncle Jack and I had not hit it off, but I felt it was his fault because of the comments he made. When we got home I told my mom; "I'm going out with the guys. I'll be back before 9.

Leonard was older than the rest of us. He was 16 and quit school to go work with his dad doing roofing and house repair stuff. His dad was cool and would let us have a beer or two in the basement.

That night, his dad had gotten us 12 beers. So it would be more than two for each of us. I drank my two and half of another. I was a little woozy, but I made it home on my bike. When I got home Jack had left and my mom was in the den doing so work for the plant. Grandma was watching TV, and Grandpa was in his room. I made sure not to get close to grandma or mom. Those two would be able to smell the beer on me. I slept okay that night, once the bed stopped spinning.

The next morning both Mom and Grandma got on my case. They had both checked in on me during the night because they said I was snoring way loud. They said that I had not fully undressed and when they came near me they could smell the beer. Nosey old women! I don't need them butting into my life.

Chapter 13

LIFE GOES ON

After speaking to Billy the way I did, I felt a little ashamed. After all he was just a kid, a little sheltered, but still a kid. During Billy's game, I thought often about the games Will and I had played on that same field, and about all the fun we would have to replay the games afterward. It finally dawned on me that Billy lacked a friend as I had in Will. I also knew that a good ballplayer always had someone they were close to. They had someone to discuss the games with and learn from.

It had been a real pleasure to watch Billy's games. He was very similar to his dad only much bigger. It had been a long time since I had watched kids playing a game for the love of the game. It was a refreshing experience.

Sharon and I had discussed a number of things during my visit. We got into the finances of the plant, and my interest in the business.

In addition, we spent time planning a trip for her, Billy and the Carter's to make a visit to Florida in a few weeks to enjoy the weather.

Sharon had told me she was worried about Billy. He was running with the wrong crowd and she had more than once smelled beer on his breath. When she asked him about it, he had said it was from drinking a half glass of beer on a bet from Leonard and his dad. She also knew that Leonard and his dad did not have the best reputation in the area and had numerous car accidents because of drinking. She asked me what I thought she could do to separate Billy from those two.

She did not care for Leonard. He was a school dropout and she had seen him smoking too. One of the biggest problems was that Leonard could get Billy to do things that Billy would not normally do on his own.

That worried me. I remembered that Will and I would dare each other to do dumb stuff like catch a ball behind our back, but aside from a beer or two when we were seniors in high school we were pretty good kids. I was at a loss as to giving Sharon any advise.

Will had once told me Sharon had gotten pissed at him when he had a beer and tried to kiss her. He said that had been his "last beer while he was with Sharon."

When I returned to Florida I told Carol and Jody about the upcoming family visit and what could we do to make them welcome?

The house was large enough for all of them to sleep comfortably. Jody and Carol would move to the "barn," which had a guest suite, so Mr. and Mrs. Carter could have their room. Billy would have one spare room, and Sharon the other. Carol arranged for some help to come in and give the place a thorough cleaning before the guests arrived. Maybe the family was right, Jody and I would not do well as bachelors.

I had Jody drive out to the airport to pick up our "company." When they got to the house they were surprised at the size of the place and the orange trees in the front yard. Plus, all the different types of oranges we were growing. Jody piped in; "And for a profit too." That was the first time I had heard we were making money from the oranges.

Jody was like a beaming proud father explaining the difference in the types of oranges and what each orange was used for; juice or eating. I was totally surprised he knew what he was talking about.

Bill was feeling the effects of the trip. I could tell that he looked worn out. Both Sharon and Lois treated Bill as a child. They forced him to sit and Carol brought the group refreshments and a bite to eat.

Carol had one of her younger sisters and a brother come by and help out for the day. Carol's brother was a student at the school where I was a coach. He was a nice young guy who doted on Jody. Jody was like a big brother to him, and he was like a younger brother to Jody. They got along great.

When the "Michiganders" arrived, Sharon pulled me aside and told me about the episode of beer drinking with Billy and his friends. She told me it was not the first time she had caught Billy drinking. She also told me that Bill was in very poor health. It was a combination of his war wounds and lung problems. The doctors had told him that he should consider retiring and moving to an area that wasn't so hard on his health.

She related that part of the reason for coming to Florida was that she and Lois had agreed to look for a place for them during the winter months in the very least. I told her that Carol was very up on the area and knew a lot of the folks in the real-estate business. Later that day, Lois, Sharon, and Carol sat down and listed out the needs of the family.

The following Monday, I asked Billy if he wanted to attend a ball practice with me. He grudgingly agreed. Once at the school, I introduced him to Coach Duane and told the coach that Billy was also a ballplayer and played on his high school JV team.

Coach Duane told Billy he could act as a ball boy for the day if he wished. Billy nodded his head, yes.

Coach called over one of the freshmen and told the ballplayer, "Take Billy here under your wing for the day. Show him around and make sure he doesn't get hurt."

After Billy went off with the freshman, Coach asked me to step into his office. He asked if I had finished my degree. He said he wanted to elevate my status to Assistant Coach from the contract position I now held. I told Duane that I had finished my degree in English studies with a minor in History. He laughed at that one. "English? Hell, you can hardly speak the language."

He then turned and said to me; "Look, Jack, I got an offer to coach a minor league team here in Florida and I've decided that I am going to take the job. I want to use it as a stepping stone to the Majors if I can. I have recommended you to be the next Head Coach. Moving you to Assistant Coach now would put you in line as my replacement when I go. Are you interested?"

"I have never given it a thought. What kind of time frame do I have before I need to give you an answer?" "Give it a week. But no longer. Spring training will be here soon and I need to be there for that."

That night I gave the offer of becoming the next Head Coach serious consideration. I decided that it was something I wanted to do. I felt I owed it to the players and myself. And, I found I was looking forward to the challenge.

Every once in a while we would look over to see how Billy was getting along with the guys. Except for having some baby fat, he looked like he belonged there. He was already nearly 6 feet tall and had some beef on him.

We watched as he got into the batting cage and was able to hit some of the pitchings from the guys. He was smart enough to alter his swing between long, hard swings and short, placement swings. Not bad for a kid!

After practice, Billy came over and was excited about the workout. It was humorous as to how he could not stop talking about "The Team" and the teammates. So I asked him; "Do you think you'd like to play college ball someday?"

"You bet Uncle Jack, at least the guys here are not treated like kids."

"Billy, you got to bear in mind, you are only 16, and have two years left in high school."

"My team is much older than you and they are responsible for themselves. Nearly all of them are on their own for the first time. Aside from that, these young men are doing their own laundry, cooking for themselves, managing their finances, and all the other things that were done for them when they were living at home. They have to take care of themselves and stay out of trouble. Their moms are not here to wake them for school, so they do everything on their own, plus, keep up with their studies."

"And keeping out of trouble is a prime thing to remember."

"Ahh! Mom told you about me drinking a beer, huh?"

"Yeah, she told me. She also said it was not the first time either. Look, Billy, I do not want to preach to you, but college coaches also select ball players for scholarships based on school grades and how mature they are. The University is not going to waste time and money on a scholarship for someone who can't contribute to the team, or someone who causes trouble with their teammates. Remember that."

When we got back to the house, Carol, Lois, and Sharon were all excited because they had found a house to look at. They wanted me to go with them but frankly, I couldn't give one hoot about seeing a house. I hadn't seen all of mine in the years that I had lived in it. So the next day, the ladies took off looking at a house and Billy and I took off for practice again.

The practice was generally the same, except today we had set up for heavy infield practice. I could read the expression on Billy's face as the players dove for balls that seemed to be out of reach. When the first baseman made a play on a ball similar to the one Billy had not played a few weeks before, Billy looked at me and smiled. Maybe he did get it after all.

One of the guys called Billy over to the batting cage. On the way over he picked up a bat. When he got to the cage the guys laughed at him, took away the bat, and told him to put on the catching gear. I could see him shaking his head "No," but the guys insisted. So he began to put on the gear. One of the catchers got him positioned behind the batter and away they went. He missed a few balls here and there and then got into the rhythm of the pitcher and batter.

Our catcher kept up a stream of conversation to him about how to hold the glove a certain way and some tips on footwork. The infield coach had told the shortstop to cover second base. Once that was set, they had Billy practice throwing the ball to second. The guys then began to teach Billy drills on throwing back to the bases to simulate pickoff plays. We called the drills "duck and cover," because you had to pay attention or you could get hit with a ball.

I asked the Infield Coach; "What are you guys doing?" Coach told me; "Look, the kid needs to learn to be a leader. He has skills, loves the game, but needs direction. Being a catcher gives him both." With that, I just smiled. My team had seen exactly what I had seen. Maybe, just maybe the kid had a chance.

That winter, my dad passed away. He had lost his final battle due to his injuries suffered during World War II and from alcoholism. So, we all packed up and went north for his funeral. Carol and Jody picked up much of the slack and things went as well as could be expected. We buried dad in the local Veterans Cemetery and his buddies from the local American Legion did the Honors Ceremony. It brought back memories of the cold day that we had buried my friend Will. Dad was well represented that day. All of his kids and grandkids were there. Nearly 74 people in total. I was the lone holdout, as to never have been married.

Upon returning home, I was amazed at the size of my younger siblings. They all seemed to grow up at once. I also visited Carter's business operation and took a tour of the plant. My brother Jay was now General Manager of Production. The plant had grown again in size and there were plans to purchase another building for future expansion.

I asked Sharon if I could take Billy out to dinner? "Just he and I. Kind of man to man." She gave me a big hug and told me it was a great idea. She added that all Billy had talked about was their time in Florida. And, that he had severed ties to his friendship with Leonard. Good news all around. Billy also began to study harder. He said he needed to get his grades up if he was going to college as his dad had done. Billy was also very proud of the fact that he was learning to be a catcher like his dad.

When we were at dinner Billy asked me question after question about his dad. What was he like as a friend? Was he a good ball player? How had Dad met his mom? And on and on. I must admit, it was great to be able to talk about my friend Will. At times I was choked up at the memories I was sharing and yet I was smiling, and the young face sitting with me was listening.

Billy reminded me so much of his dad, my best friend Will. He also asked if he could come back to Florida to be with the team. As much as I would like him there I told him he needed to be with his own teammates to form the bonds required to be winners.

I spent some time with my mom and got her to agree to visit us in Florida. I think the clincher was that my sister June and sister-in-law, Beth said they would travel with her. Once we were sure they were coming down, I hired a local firm recommended by Jody and Carol to install an in-ground pool and redo the patio area. I told Beth that she needed to bring the kids with her and we would plan a trip to Disney World for the family.

The Carter's business was now going great guns. It was still a family business, owned by majority between the Carter family and my family, the Tyler's.

Another of my brothers, Jerry started to work in the plant after getting out of the Air Force and graduating from college. He was working his way up to be Jay's, right-hand man.

My mom was a worry wart. She had worried all the way down to Florida about her first plane ride and then began to worry about the kids still at home. We all started kidding her and then she seemed to relax a bit. She loved the house and giggled a lot when she was able to pick an orange off of a tree in the backyard to eat.

Mom got real serious and told me she had not done that since she was in California when my dad was stationed there during the war. She told me how, when I was a baby I used to roll the oranges on the ground toward my brother and he would roll them back to me. I guess that was my first game of catch.

My niece, Nicole was now 15 and was a very nice young lady. Lucky for her, she favored her mom in looks. I asked her if she and Billy were still good friends and all she did was let out a grunt. She did add the comment that "all Billy thinks about is playing ball and working on old cars." So much for that. Nicole spent most of her visit by the pool, except for the two-day visit to Disney World.

While the family was here, I tried to convince my mom to come down for the winters and stay for a few months or at least a few weeks. She told me she would see how it goes.

Later that winter, I received a phone call from Billy telling me about the baseball camp he had attended and all the attention he had gotten from college coaches. I told him, "Tell them to bug off. You'll play for me, or play for no one!" I was smiling from ear to ear with the news.

Billy asked if I could find an old car for him to rebuild because he was going to driver's education and wanted to fix up his own car. I told him I would look around. I asked Billy when he had his American League baseball schedule to send me a copy so I could see if the schedule my team had would match the same time period when we came in town to play some of the (MAC) Mid America Conference teams.

During that summer, my team traveled to Michigan as part of our schedule and I was able to watch Billy and his teammates play a weekend tournament. A few of my players went with me to watch and spent some of the game razzing Billy every time he was involved in a play. You could see that he was the best player on the field. He crushed the ball each time he batted and threw a runner out at third on an attempted steal. In the stands, I could see some of the local college coaches watching the game. It was very apparent which ballplayer they were scouting.

That night we had a combined dinner, the Tyler family and the Carter family. During the dinner, I could see the attraction between Billy and (my niece) Nicole. It brought back memories of the romance between Will and Sharon at that age. Later that evening Billy and I finally had a few minutes to talk. We mostly spoke about how my search was going to find him an old car to rebuild.

Later that winter, I resolved myself to get in gear and find the car for Billy so he would have something to keep him busy when he came to Florida to visit. I first looked through the want ads, then I went around to the dealerships to see what had been taken in trade. One dealer representative told me of an old scrap yard where the owner only dealt in vehicles from the '30s, '40s, and '50s. He also told me that a good place to find old cars that were in excellent shape was through estate sales. So I started checking estate sales and auction houses for estate auctions.

The drive to the yard was about an hour away, so I saved the drive for another day. Busy teaching a class on freshman composition, I had forgotten the car search. Sharon called early one morning and told me the family was coming down for the winter and she asked if I could find someone to open the house for them.

After chatting for a few minutes, we said goodbye and then I realized I now had two assignments to get done.

So, I called Carol and told her about my dilemma and she just laughed. She told me that she had a company that did just that; opened and refreshed houses and condos for families returning to Florida for the winter. Okay, thanks to Carol, one assignment was done. Now for the old car search.

Chapter 14

PAST & PRESENT BECOME FUTURE

It was the following Spring before I was formally offered the position as Head Coach and I gladly accepted. I had spent the previous season as the interim coach when Coach Duane had moved on to coach in the minor leagues. In addition to the head coaching position, I was also required to teach at least one class at the school. I thought that I could and would do well as an American English professor.

Most of my ballplayers came from Florida, with a few from the surrounding area and states. I had planned a recruiting meeting for a local kid that was close to the scrap yard, so I set up the meeting and figured I could kill two birds with one stone. Just prior to my trip, I was asked to drop in and see the Athletic Director for a few minutes. He needed to see me about an appointment he was about to make.

The AD and I had very little contact except when he attended the games that we played at home. He attended a few of the local away games, but seldom went outside the state. We, the coaches at the university thought it was a great relationship. He allowed us to run our programs as we saw fit. Once in a while, he would step in to ensure we knew who was the boss.

The AD welcomed me into his office and asked me to sit down and relax. He offered me a soft drink and asked how I thought the team was going to do in the upcoming season.

After a few minutes of small talk there was a knock on the door and the AD's Admin Kat stuck her head in the door and said; "Sir the Trainer is here to see you"

"Great! Send Eddie in to meet Coach Jack."

In walked a young woman, most likely a few years younger than me. But it was difficult to tell. She was very pretty, average height and had beautiful flaming red hair.

Jack, this is Eddie Paulson. She is a Physical Trainer. Eddie recently retired from the Navy and decided to stay here in Florida while her kids finished school. We were lucky to intercept her and hire her as an athletic trainer. I would consider it a favor if you could show her around the campus. Her new duties will include working with your team."

As I turned to shake Eddie 's hand, a glimmer of recognition crept into my head. I was not sure where it came from, but it was there.

Eddie turned to me and said; "The AD tells me you were in the Army." Then she said, "Oh my God! You're Staff Sergeant Tyler! I was a nurse at Great Lakes when you first came home from Vietnam. I think I gave you a shave once, right?"

I was speechless, the memories came flooding back to me. The time in the hospital, the work toward recovery and the night I received the news of Will's death. All I could think to do was to sit down. My mind had locked up.

Eddie walked over and said, "Coach are you okay? Do you need a glass of water?"

"No. I am okay. It was just a shock to see someone from my past. From that part of my life. How have you been? Edwina, right?"

"I have been doing very well Coach. I just recently retired from the Navy."

"Oh, what a surprise! I am just stunned to see you here."

"Well here I am, and I must say, you look much better than the last time I saw you."

"Yeah, I was in bad shape back then. But thanks to you and the others, I made it through and was able to get on with my life."

After outlining what contribution Eddie would lend the athletic department, the AD said: "Well you two, I see that you already know each other. So, get on your way and get back to me if there is anything else I can do to help you with your duties."

At that, the AD ushered us out of his office and into the outer office space where Kat said a few words to Eddie. "Mrs. Paulson, there are a few items I need for you to complete. Take them with you and get them back to me in a few days."

"Yes, ma'am. I will get them right back to you tomorrow."

"Okay Coach! Where's the first stop on our tour?"

"Please, just call me Jack. I was thinking we should get lunch and I can explain the campus to you. How's that sound? By the way, isn't your last name the same as the Doctor from Great Lakes, Dr. Paulson?"

"Yes, he and I were married. But only a few people knew it at the time."

"So how is the Doc?" He was very good to me while I was there."

"The Doc and I parted ways some years ago. He likes nurses, but the young ones. And as you can see, I am not that sweet, young, Texas nurse anymore."

"Mrs. Paulson you look great. Much better than I do for your age."

"I mean, you look a lot younger than me but…."

"It's okay Jack. I know what you mean. And please, just call me Eddie."

We stopped at the cafeteria and ate our lunch, discussing the guys we could remember from Great Lakes. She told me that some of the patients got together in a sort of loose reunion. There had been a few from time to time over the past 20 years or so.

"As we went through the list of names, I remember getting the note from your brother on the passing of your close friend Will. You remember having one of the nurses sew your patches on your uniform?"

"Yeah, I do remember. But I never told her "thank you."

"You just did, soldier. You just did."

"Come on Eddie. I'll show you your new digs. Are you familiar with the campus at all?"

"Yes, somewhat. My two kids go to school here. The youngest, my daughter, is a new freshman and the eldest, my son is a pre-med student."

"So how long have you been living here?"

"Actually, I do not live here yet. I am still looking for a place. Right now I am staying at a local hotel. My kids are in the dorms. How about you Jack? Any kids, wife, that kind of thing?"

"Nope. Never got around to getting married. Come to think of it, I never even got close. Hey! Would you like to have dinner with me tonight?"

"Well, I'd love to. It certainly would beat eating alone again. The kids have their own "things" going on and they don't want to be bothered with their Mom hovering around."

"Okay, I'll make a quick call, and we'll be on our way."

"Breaking a date?"

"Nope, just letting my brother and sister-in-law know about our plans. Let's go! Do you have a car and want to follow me? Or do you want me to drive?"

"Where are we going to eat?"

"I just told them that I was bringing you home for dinner. The next worse thing from eating alone is to eat restaurant food with me."

On the way over to the farm, we chatted a bit about what Eddie's duties would be concerning the ball team. Once we got to the farm, we were met in the driveway by Jody and Carol. As we got out of the car, I could see Carol talking in Jody's ear.

Carol hurried to us and said; "Hi, I'm Carol. So glad to meet you! I'm Jack's sister-in-law, and this other Bozo here is Jack's brother, Jody."

"And you are Eddie? Jack said on the phone he was bringing the new trainer named Eddie. But you're a girl. Well, I mean a woman!"

"Yes. I am a woman," she said with a giggle. "I just retired from the Navy where I had been a nurse, in the beginning, then a physical therapist and a trainer. My kids go to college here and I saw an advertisement for a position. Since that's my specialty, I applied, and got the job."

The two ladies walked arm and arm toward the house and left Jack and Jody staring and bewildered, behind them.

"So welcome to our home Eddie. And, how are you getting along with Jack?"

"Very well. He's a kind, gentle person. You don't know this, but Jack and I met each other in the past. I was a nurse when he came to the hospital at Great Lakes, during the Vietnam War."

"Oh Really?" inquired Carol with a surprised look on her face.

"Yes. We lost touch after he went home on leave. Right after his friend died in Vietnam."

"That was a very sad time in Jack's life. He has never really seemed to get over it. Jody and I sometimes hear him talking to his friend Will while he's sleeping."

"Well, come on in the house. It will be nice to have another women join in the conversation. Sometimes I feel outnumbered with those two characters. Dinner's almost ready."

When the girls went into the house, Jody started in on me with the twenty questions. I told him; "Back off brother. She is an employee, just like me. Someone that I briefly knew in my past. That's it."

Dinner went well. The girls acted as if they were lifelong friends, and Carol seemed very happy to have another woman to converse with instead of just Jody and I.

When I told them that I needed to get Eddie back to her place, Carol told me that she would drive Eddie back so I could get some rest.

"Okay by me. "By the way Eddie, I have a recruiting stop to make tomorrow, if you are interested in going along for the drive. I think it would be good for you to observe the process."

"Sure, that would be great. What time will you pick me up?"

"How about 10 am sharp?"

"That should work just fine for me. Thanks!"

The next morning as we drove, we got reacquainted. Eddie told me that she had retired as a Lt. Commander and aside from a small Navy pension, she would need to work to supplement her income. We stopped at the potential student's home and spoke to him and his parents. It was nice having Eddie with me, that way I would not have to carry the whole conversation by myself. She was also able to give the family a different slant on the college life, and she could answer questions from a parent's point of view.

The recruits mom asked me; "If I were a parent, would I send my children to that school?" She was concerned with the types of groups and activities he could get involved in, both good and bad. Eddie broke in and added that she had two kids attending school there and she was very happy with the classes and the campus. She also added a few things like; church groups and study groups that were available to students as well.

When we got back into the car, I asked Eddie; "Where did you learn about the church and study groups?"

"Jack, I just read that in the brochures that the college puts out for the students."

After the meeting we went over to the car lot, aka junkyard, to see if I could find a suitable car for Billy to rebuild when he comes down for the summer.

I settled on a 1950 Ford, small window coupe. Years ago, when I was a kid, we called those car body types "Doctor's Coupes." The Fords of those years were also called shoe box cars because the body style resembled a shoe box. I picked that car because of the old flathead engine. They were very easy to work on, and the body sheet metal was one of the last thick gauge, steel bodies. The owner wanted $550. I got him to settle on five hundred dollars, and he would deliver the car to my house.

On the way home Eddie and I stopped and ate dinner and she asked me about the car and what were my plans for it?

I explained to her who Billy was, and about our relationship. I told her that he was on his way down from Michigan after his ball season was over and that he was thinking of going to school down here to play baseball.

She asked me, "So, what kind of kid is he? How old is he? Is he a good student?"

I told her; "Whoa, he's too young for you to date."

"Not for me, silly! I was thinking of my daughter because she doesn't make friends easily and can be domineering. And the friends she does make, have one thing in common. They can not look her straight in the eye and say NO!. She is only seventeen and younger than the rest of her classmates. Plus, she is a little shy. So how tall is he?"

"How Tall? Why would that matter?"

"Because my daughter is nearly six feet tall and she can be a little intimidating because of that. She needs people who can look her in the eye and say NO!"

"Well, Billy is kind of used to that from his mother. The last time I saw Billy he was taller than me and I am nearly 6'3"."

"So, what is your relationship with Billy's mother?"

"We've been close friends and confidants since we were 11 years old. She was my best friend's girlfriend and then wife. For the two of us, it's never gone any further than that."

I dropped Eddie off at her motel and told her that I'd see her at work the following day.

A few days later, the old Ford showed up, I set out to clean it out and wash it down before starting any restoration work on it.

Jody and I got to work on the Ford and discussed what had been going on in our lives since we last had a few minutes together. He told me that he and Carol were thinking of buying out the neighboring farm and extending the orange groves. They were also thinking of growing grapes in some areas that were decently shaded. He said that their business interests were doing well and that at some point they would be moving into their own place.

The following week, Eddie brought her two kids Tom and Beverly out for dinner and to have a dip in the pool. You could tell the kids were related. They were both tall and slim and had their mom's red hair. Eddie had been right about one thing with her daughter, she was very reserved. Her son was older by a few years and was looking forward to his last year at med school.

The kids were interested to hear about their parents from someone from the past. I prefaced that I could relate what I could, but because of my injuries and my somewhat faulty memory, it would not be much. As I told my story you could see the sadness in their eyes.

Tom remarked that it was a shame as to what the Vietnam Vets, had to go through at such a young age. Beverly just sat and looked at me. You could see the tears forming at the edges of her eyes. When I saw the beginnings of those tears, I decided it was time to cut it short and move on to happier things. I told the kids that they were welcome to come out at any time, especially on the weekends so they would not need to stay at the dorms or sit around their Mom's small motel room.

Eddie asked if the invitation extended to her. "Oh, sorry. Sure!" I said. "The invite includes you. In fact, you are welcome to take up residence in the guest house if you want. It would help solve a dilemma I am having and save you some money on your rent."

"Oh? What dilemma are you having?"

"Carol and Jody are going to move out soon and I hate being alone. Knowing someone is nearby would help."

"Okay, let me think about it for a few days."

Beverly looked at her mom and said; "Mom, it's the deal of a lifetime for you. You should do it. Besides I love the pool."

"Well, if I was in your guest house, I would insist on paying rent. How about I pay you the same amount I'm paying at the Residence Inn? And I would like to sign a lease if that is okay with you?

"It is fine by me. I'll have Carol draw up a lease agreement. In the meantime, let's plan a date when we can move you in. I'll ask Jody to give us a hand. Maybe Tom can help out too."

About a week later, the plan came together and we moved Eddie into the guest house.

A month later, the Carters came down. They called from their place after they arrived and we made a date for dinner together in a few days, allowing them time to get settled in.

When Billy heard I had gotten him a car, he insisted on coming right over to see it. Aside from cleaning and washing the car, I had not touched it.

When Billy saw the car, he thought it was the most beautiful car he had ever seen. He walked around the car waving his hands and talking about all the plans he had to make it a cool ride.

I just stood there and smiled. He sounded just like me at that age. Then I gave him the bad news. We could work on the car in the yard, but the Florida sun would take a toll on us. He just looked at me like, huh? I told him we would have to build some

type of cover to protect ourselves and any progress we made on the car.

The next day we sat down and created a work plan. I told him "we wanted to do a number of things to the car, but we also want it to be modern under the outer skin."

I told Billy that I had planned to have a garage built at some time, so I just accelerated the plan. So now, we would have a cover to work on the car.

Next, I hired a concrete company to come over to pour the footings and floor. And two weeks later, the carpenters arrived and put up the building. One of my English students was an older guy who had worked as a roofer, so I hired him to install the roof. During the garage build time, Eddie got to know Billy and I was surprised that they got along so well.

That day, during the drive to the university Eddie, told me, "I like Billy, I think he will be a good friend for Beverly. She has never made friends too easily."

"Have you talked to Beverly about this? And maybe Sharon?"

"Sure. Sharon and I have had a few conversations about it already."

"When did all of this happen?"

"When you and Billy were working on the car."

"Dare I ask what other plots you two have dreamed up?"

"Not yet," she said with a smile.

Chapter 15

BILLY JACK

The ball season in Michigan had ended. We had lost the high school championship game. It was a very tough loss for us, although the game was close it was still a loss. I then began to think about getting down to Florida and seeing Uncle Jack. I knew they played ball year-round in Florida and some of the nations top players were from Florida. If I could, I was hoping to catch on with a team and improve my ball skills.

Prior to the Michigan tournament, two of our pitchers came up with tender arms and just could not throw during the tournament week. I pitched a few innings but that left our catching to a freshman. He was pretty good but lacked the stamina to go the whole tournament. When he tired, his hitting fell off and then his defense.

Coach Jack told my mom that if I enrolled early and took two summer classes I could qualify for fall baseball at school. Therefore, I would not need to find another team. I could play for Coach Jack. I was all for that. So before we left for Florida, Mom helped me register for two classes. One was Freshman English, the second was a Humanities class. Both classes were requirements toward a degree.

Between working on the car, baseball practice and classes, I did not have much free time. Coach Jack had a nice lady who also worked at the university renting the guest house. Her name was Eddie. She worked at the university as an athletic trainer. She talked to me about the various stretching exercises I could do to increase my flexibility. I didn't really know much about what she was saying, but I agreed to try some of the stretching exercises.

After about two weeks I noticed that my swing was looser than it had been. The looser swing meant that my bat was quicker. I also noticed that my legs did not cramp up as much and some of the soreness had disappeared. So maybe those exercises had a positive effect on my skills.

At practice, I noticed one of the senior players joking with Coach Jack just prior to my turn in the cage. Coach then went to the bench and got his glove and went to the mound.

He hollered at me, "Okay kid, let's see if you can hit an old man."

The rest of the team stopped to watch. It was me and Uncle Jack. I had no idea as to what was coming. He started slow. Easy fastballs in the mid 60's range and then increased the speed as his arm loosened up. The next few pitches had to be in the low 80's and then I knew I was in a battle with someone who could best me at my game. It was touch and go if I could hit the ball. I hit a few solid and fouled off more that. Finally, I could hit solid however, I could not hit anything with power. At that point, I was just trying not to swing and miss.

Just as I got the timing down, Coach increased the speed again. High 80's I figured. I hit one pitch real good and was waiting for the next one with a big smile on my face. I waited for the pitch, poised to really give it a ride. To my considerable surprise, the pitch broke right in on my hands and I hit the ball weakly toward first base. He had thrown me a slider. I had been so intent on hitting the fastball, I had not paid attention to what the actual pitch had been. Lesson one; I had been a victim of my own making.

Coach Jack gave me a big smile and walked off the mound toward the plate. "Not bad, for a rookie."

The rest of the team yelled at me, whistled and laughed.

One of the team captains said to me; "Kid you have just been initiated. Welcome to big time baseball."

He then said; "Coach does that to all the rookies. At least you hit the ball."

Coach Jack disappeared and the assistant coaches finished up the practice. Because the guys had played summer ball, the league we were in included a few of the bigger schools and a few low minor league teams. That was part of the reason I wanted to play down here. The opportunity for great competition. When we finished up, I went looking for Jack to catch my ride home.

I found him in the trainer's room getting his arm iced down. He had his back to the door and I could see small drops of blood on his back. Just before I was going to say something sarcastic, I thought better of it. Along with the small drops of blood, his back was full of scars. It looked more like a road map with the roads heading in many directions. So I asked, "Coach, you ready to go home?"

"Yup, I'm ready. You wore me out."

"You do know you have blood on your back?"

"Ah, hell! Ask Eddie to come in here and give me a hand."
Eddie came in with a set of tweezers. "Another one, huh?"

"Yup, another one, or two or three."

Eddie got to work. She removed some things from Jack's back and then rubbed the spots down with alcohol.

"All done, she said."

I asked what any young kid would ask: "What was causing the blood; and what were those scars?"

"Those scars were a result of me getting hit by shrapnel during my time in Vietnam. Little pieces of metal come to the surface from time to time."

"Do they hurt?"

"Not now, but they certainly did when I first got them." And he just chuckled.

Eddie added; "I knew your Uncle back then. I was a nurse in the hospital when they first brought him back from Vietnam. He certainly looks much better now than he did back then. I knew him when he was one tough cookie, not the pushover he is now."

"What was he like back then?"

"I'll tell you some other time. Okay?"

When we got back to Uncle Jack's and got out of the car, I could hear voices from the backyard pool area. Eddie said, "I think the kids are here. And, isn't that Sharon's car?"

"Yeah, that looks like hers. And that other car is a rental. I think the gang's all here."

When we got around to the back of the house there was my Mom, Grandma, Grandpa, Jody, Carol, and Jay with his kids, and two other young people I didn't know.

Eddie said to me, "Billy, those two are my kids. Tom and Beverly. Come on over and I will introduce them to you."

Tom was in a deep conversation with Nicole and didn't even notice us walk up. His sister stood up when we got to the side of the pool and in my mind, I thought; "Whoa! She is really tall."

Beverly held out her hand and shook mine. Her brother broke away from Nicole and also shook my hand. Tom was as tall as me but slimmer. Beverly was shorter than me, but not by much. I looked at her eyes. They were beautiful. Green with just a touch of gold. She was a redhead, the dark red that was between brown and black. What a beauty. I looked from her to her mom and back. Yeah, they were certainly mother and daughter.

Just as I was about to take a deeper look at Bev, (I had resolved to call her Bev and not Beverly) my mom came over and said; "Billy. you should go inside and clean up a bit. You smell like old sweat socks."

"Okay, Mom. I just need to say hello to the rest of the folks first, okay?

I was then off to say hello to Grandma and Grandpa. I figured a wave to the rest would be okay.

Uncle Jack and his brother Jody were gathered at my old Ford. I could see they were offering tips on how the car should be finished. Seeing that I traveled back and forth to school with Uncle Jack on most days, I had a stash of clothes at his house. I had discussed moving to his house, but the idea was vetoed by my mom. She wanted me at her place when she was down in Florida.

I jumped in the shower, then slipped on a t-shirt and a pair of shorts. I went back outside where Jody was cooking on the grill, preparing dinner. The rest of the guys were gathered around the grille with beers in their hands.

Nicole came over to me and said; "Isn't he a great looking guy?"

I said, "Who are you talking about?"

"Tom! I think he is so cute."

So I asked Nicole, "What do you think about his sister Beverly?"

"Oh, she's okay. Kind of skinny though."

During dinner, I found out that to save more money on dorm fees, the two kids had come to stay with their mom at the guest house. The younger set fell into a routine where once I got home from school or ball games we would take a dip in the pool and do a little work on the Ford. I also thought it was cool that Bev would help with the Ford when we worked on it. She did not know a lot about tools, but she was interested in how things were put together. She seemed to catch onto things real fast.

When we had out of town games or night games, I would skip the pool and the car work. I opted for shut eye, so sometimes I did not see Bev or Tom for a few days at a time.

We were like a family. Jack and Eddie would watch us in the pool. We ate dinner and then went to our separate houses to sleep for the night. To me, it was a wonderful time. Bev and Tom became like a brother and sister to me, which I had never had. I also found that when I was around then, I acted a little more mature. They were both excellent students and very polite.

Slowly I started to fall for Bev. She was remarkable. Beautiful and smart. She was following the same pre-med study course as her brother Tom and wanted to be a doctor. She certainly had the smarts to do so. Tom had secured a residency program in the nearby hospital and was not always here, so Bev and I were able to spend more time together, alone and we got to know each other even better.

On rare occasions, Bev and I would borrow her Mom's car, or Uncle Jack's. Then we would go into town for a fast food meal and ice cream. If Bev did not have classes when we played a home game, she would attend my ball games. Her mom would also come to some of the games when she was not attending other games that the college was involved in.

It was a good "family time" for us. Bev became more interested in our games and admitted it was the first time she had any interest in sports. She told me she was kind of nerdy in high school and being a military kid they had moved around some and she did not have many opportunities to make close friends.

Many nights, Bev and I were alone. I behaved myself and she certainly did too. But, it was getting more difficult day by day to be a gentleman.

I was learning a ton of stuff from the coaches. It seemed as if Jack had hired coaches who had expertise in different aspects of the game. And all of them were good teachers.

The infield coach taught us things like how to pick up the other teams signs and how to switch off base coverages so that the other team could not take advantage of you moving on a hit and run play. The outfield coach taught us things like how to decoy a runner so the runner would not or could not take an extra base on a hit. We were taught how to read the other coaches signs on what pitch was going to be thrown by the pitcher. The learning seemed to go on and on. I was eating it up!

Jack had me on the bench most of the first three games. I was told to sit between him and the infield coach and listen to them talk about the pace and tenor of the game. In some ways, I began to think like they did, except I was much more aggressive in my thoughts.

During the third game, Jack told me in the fourth inning that I would pinch hit for the pitcher the next time he came up. Jack wanted to give the pitcher a rest and get me and another freshman pitcher in the game. He asked me if I knew what the other pitcher was going to throw me?

"You mean like what kind of pitch?"

"Yeah, that's what I mean."

"I am not sure."

"Think about what he starts all the batters off with and how he has worked the strike zone."

"He has thrown the left handed hitters up and in and the right-hand hitter down and away. Not always fast balls, but pitch locations."

"Good, good! I think you're ready. Now, go get him!"

The third base coach gave me the take sign on the first two pitches. The first was a slider up and in. The second was another slider down and in that was so low the catcher needed to block it. I stepped out of the box, took a blow and the coach gave me the go sign and indicated that the pitch would be belt high over the outside black of the plate. I was ready!

The pitch was almost exactly where it was supposed to be. Slightly below the belt. On the outside black. I got a little too aggressive and fouled the pitch behind third base. Two balls and one strike. I figured the next pitch would be a slider, either down and in or high and tight.

The third base coach gave me the sign that loosely said: "you're on your own" and he smiled. I looked at the bench and Jack looked me in the eye and gave the same sign.

The next pitch was knee high and a little middle in. I put a good strong swing on the ball and it was over the right field fence before I got to first base. GONE!! My first college hit had been a home run.

As I rounded the bases the team began to tease me. By the time I got to third, I heard the chants; "Billy Jack! Billy Jack!!" I know I was smiling from ear to ear.

When I got back to the bench, Jack said to me, "Nice rap, but you missed the bunt sign."

"No, I saw the Go Sign!"

"Just funning you. Nice rap!"

The rest of the season was a good one for the team and me. Jack used his players wisely. He gave them all great opportunities to succeed. He played all of his players and the baseball education was more than I had ever thought possible. I did get to catch some of the games and between innings.

Jack and the other coaches would talk to me about our pitchers and ask things like "did they still have enough gas? And were their pitches still breaking as they should?" There was always baseball talk on the bench. All the guys got into it. Even the outfielders were interested in what the infielders were doing. Like when they were playing a step to the right or left for certain hitters. The infielders then got into discussions on how they would adjust the cut off positions to save time.

We played a ton of ball games. Jack would schedule scrimmages with any team that would play against us. Coach Jack was not shy about scheduling games with Division 1 teams. He'd told us" if you want to be the best, you gotta play the best."

Jack and all the coaches were sticklers for classroom work. They would get on your ass if your grades slipped. Since I had such a close relationship with Jack, I kept my grades way up above average. Between the games, scrimmages, and workouts, I had very few hours left to work on the Ford and to see Bev.

I remember mentioning to Jack that I had not seen Bev for almost a week while on a ride home one night and I remember his reply. "There will be plenty of time for romance once you are established."

"Like you Uncle Jack?"

"Yeah, like me."

The second season of regular ball, the team was on a tear. The pitchers were at the top of their game and the defense was solid as a rock. I had moved up to first string catcher and caught most of the innings. Jack would have me DH when the games were under American League rules. He told me he did it for a variety of reasons. The other catchers also needed to get some experience to develop, plus he also said he was preparing for the day I would no longer be on the team. I did not pay much attention to what my batting average was or the other stats related to my hitting, but I did know I only had one game where I was hit-less.

I enjoyed the scrimmages against the minor league teams the best. Their pitchers were better and threw more strikes. I learned real quick that when these pitchers missed the strike zone and or wanted to miss, they could hit spots that were un-hitable. Very few of them missed over the center of the plate.

My nick name evolved from Billy Jack to Black Jack. I guess it had to do with my black catching equipment. I kinda played along and painted a skull and crossbones on my mask. I was having the time of my life!

We had a great team both on and off the field. Having fun as a description was not even close to describing the good times we had. Because of my class load and the fact that I had played two college years, I was considered to be a Junior. That alone did not mean much to me except I only had two years remaining of college eligibility to play ball.

My mom was pushing me to make a decision as to a solid major in studies. I was leaning towards engineering, although I needed to increase my science classes. So being the smart guy that I was, I asked Bev what classes she thought I needed to take that would get me to my goal, but without cramping my upcoming baseball season.

Bev helped me identify a few classes, so I registered for those classes. And I finally had time to get to work on the old Ford.

Chapter 16

Billy's Dream

In the spring of Billy's sophomore year, the Major Leagues held their annual amateur draft. The majors would run through all the scouting reports and the rosters of their minor leagues to determine the current and future need. Pitching and catching are always needed so those amateur players are always at a premium. On the day the draft was being held Billy began to get phone calls. The first one was from the Detroit Tigers asking if Billy would consider signing a pro-contract and forgo his last two years of college. Billy told them that he would consider signing a contract if the terms were right.

To Billy's surprise, he was drafted at the beginning of the second round by the Detroit Tigers. In addition, three of Billy's teammates were also drafted by other clubs. When The four young men got to school that day they sat down and had a BS session about being drafted. For the most part, they thought it was cool, but could not fathom being pro ball players.

Billy noticed that the phone calls kept coming. The local newspapers were also on the story. Baseball was king in Florida. The newspapers played up the fact that no other college team had ever had four players taken in the same draft. Billy called the other guys to discuss what they would say to the increased pressure of the media for comments, "I would suggest that we all echoed the same theme; that they had Coach Jack to thank for that because of his coaching and leadership skills in forming a team that truly believed in teamwork and helping the team win."

Most of the attention went towards our "Big Horse" right-handed pitcher, Jimmy Paul, and I was thankful for that. Aside from being a great pitcher, he was very quotable and could talk for hours and not make a bit of sense. Many compared him to the one time Tiger pitcher Mark Fitzgerald.

That evening Mom, Jack and I, all sat down to discuss the options I had. Surprisingly, Jack favored me taking some time to make my decision. He suggested I finish up this semester at school, as he said, "to better prepare myself for life without/after baseball."

Mom, for the most part, wanted me to follow my dream, but reminded me that "opportunities come and go." She also wanted to talk to Gramps before I did anything that would close doors on other opportunities I may have in the future within the structure of the family business.

"Billy," she said "you have plenty of time to make a decision. Don't rush it."

"Have you spoken to Beverly about it?"

"Beverly?"

"Why?"

"Oh!

About a week later the Tigers called and asked for a conference with me and my mom. I asked if they would mind if I had Uncle Jack attend. The Tigers said they had no problem with Jack being included in the conversations. The Tigers even suggested that being a former pro ball player may be an advantage in having Jack there with us.

We met at Mom's place and the Tigers made it clear that they really wanted to get me signed and get me on my way to the rookie ball before the season ended in a few months. They wanted me to get into the organization and begin the transformation from college to pro-ball. One of the reps commented that pro-ball was a lot more detailed than what I had encountered during college.

"Then you have never played for Coach Jack." That got a few chuckles from everyone in the room.

"Right! And part of the reason we drafted you is that we are 100% sure that Coach Jack prepares his players for greater things. So let's get down to business."

I was amazed at how much my mother changed during these discussions. She looked like my Mom but was like a true negotiator during the discussions. I guess her years of experience in negotiating contracts for the plant taught her some skills I never realized she possessed. She had a lot of great questions I never would have thought of like what if this or what if that happens? And would the club pay for me to finish college?

Uncle Jack also asked a lot of great questions pertaining to baseball and the kind of vision the Tigers had for me in the future. Many were things I wouldn't have thought to ask. I just knew I wanted to play pro ball.

At one point Uncle Jack turned and said to me; "Billy, you are making a life-changing decision. We want you to have no regrets. If things do not fit into your vision, you can always come back to school and wait till the next draft to go pro."

At that point, the Tiger rep broke in and began to offer assurances as to what the Tigers had planned for me. It included time off in the winter to attend classes, and tickets for the family to watch me play at Tiger Town in Lakeland, Florida. (Lakeland is the home of the Detroit Tigers spring training and their rookie team, the Lakeland Tigers.)

The Tigers had a legal court reporter take down the entire meeting so that there would not be a misunderstanding to the conditions of any contract in the future.

When we had concluded the meeting, I saw Uncle Jack nod at Mom and she said; "Well gentlemen, thanks for the visit and the interesting conversation. Please have your legal department send over a written offer and we will take it into serious consideration." Then she added: "If it is possible, would you also included a transcript of what we discussed here today?"

"Oh course Mrs. Carter, we will include it with the written offer. And, I must say it has been a pleasure to speak to all of you and I would hope we can see each other in a more relaxed setting in the near future. Maybe when Billy hits his first homer for the Tigers."

After the meeting was over, I went to see Beverly. I wanted to get some input from her. I kinda needed to know what her thoughts were about our future together and what it would be like if I went off to play ball.

Bev and I talked about me going away and what we might miss being separated. Then she asked me the big question. "What difference does it make what and how I feel about you being gone?"

"Well, I thought we had something going as a couple."

"Well do we? What do you think we have together? What do you feel about our relationship?"

"Ah gee, you know how I feel about you."

"Do I? Have you ever said anything about your feelings or asked me how I felt about you?"

"Billy we are dating. Yet we are almost like brother and sister. My brother Tom and Nicole are further along in a relationship than we are."

"Come on, you know how I feel about you."

"Okay. Tell me."

"Well, I think I love you, Bev."

"You think?"

That's when I took her hand and looked her straight in the eye and said; "Bev, I do love you and I don't want to lose you over this."

"Billy, I thank you for that. It sure took you long enough to say it! And just so you know, I love you too, and I have been in love with you for years."

"Okay! So, what's next?"

"I think we need to talk to our parents."

The next day we had the talk with our parents and everyone had big smiles on their faces. think it may have been the first time I had seen my mom ever smile like that. Mom and Eddie even hugged each other.

I wanted to get Bev an engagement ring but she told me she did not need a ring, but she would take the title on my Ford as an engagement present. I was totally dumbfounded. Then she began to laugh with her mom and my mom. I was kinda relieved. I loved that old Ford.

A few days later I asked Mom to come over to Jack's house for dinner and we all sat around and talked about what the future could be. As we talked, it became clear that I did want to sign and play pro ball.

About a week later, a special messenger brought over the contract along with the transcript they had promised.

In the envelope, there was also a note from the Tigers requesting that I "come over to Tiger Town and do an official signing for the media?"

We set up a time for the signing on a day that the major league club had an exhibition game.

The Tigers wanted to have their major league manager there for the signing and have him hold a Tiger jersey as I slipped it on.

On the day of signing, we drove over to Tiger Town and I was very nervous. The rest of our small party seemed to be very relaxed. My mom said the decision has already been made and there was no sense in being nervous now.

The press conference and signing went without a hitch. The Tiger manager said something about wanting to "get my bat in the lineup as soon as possible."

A few of the people at the signing knew Jack from years ago and his history as a college coach. So for Uncle Jack, it was kinda like an old home week.

Later, we sat around in the owners club seats and watched the game. The GM/General Manager sat next to me and kept a steady banter about the club and how they were expected to compete for the Central Division crown that season.

The GM asked me what I thought of the club. Thinking I should be honest, I told him that I thought third in the division was about the limit. He asked where I had come up with that? I told him, "My Uncle Jack and I discussed the club last night and we agree that may be the limit."

"Tell me, what do you see are the clubs limitations?"

"You need relief pitching, a middle infielder, and an upgrade in center field. And your catcher has some age on him."

"Well young man, you may be right, but keep that to yourself, okay?

"Yes, Sir." I had learned another baseball lesson, just be quiet and do your job. "Thou does not speak ill of your ball club."

We spent the night in Lakeland and the folks left right after breakfast but I stayed in Lakeland. I now had a job to do.

I took a cab over to the field and was surprised that there were only a few guys in the clubhouse suiting up.

I went over to the equipment manager to pick up a uniform and some used catching gear. The club told me they would order some new gear based on what gear I favored. In the meantime, I would use what had been left behind by one of the players that had been cut.

The clubhouse manager told me there were a few numbers left, and asked: "did I have a preference?"

"What are the numbers?"

"We have; 10, 44, 55, 67, and 99."

"Okay, how about 55? It kinda sounds like a catcher's number."

Okay, number 55 it is. You got it!"

A few minutes later, the coaches began to show up on the field and they split us up into position groups. When that was done, they picked out a few guys and told them to get loose and then get over to the main field. They were going to be the reserves for the parent club during the game today. Those fellows selected were thrilled. They acted like kids at Christmas.

I was wondering why there were so many guys in our group when the catching coach came over and took me aside. He introduced himself and told me that the minor league guys worked out and practiced together until they were assigned to clubs. Being assigned to a club meant that you were being assigned according to your current skill levels and the needs of the ball club.

Aside from me, there was only one other rookie signee. He was a local kid like me, but he was right out of high school.

The practice was a little easier than it had been at school, but I soon realized they were trying to avoid injuries. For me, it was my first workout in a couple of days, but the others had been at it for less than a week and were not baseball ready.

We went into a building at the rear of the complex and had batting practice. I also worked with some of the pitchers. During the workout, the catching instructor kept asking me questions about   my technique and questions like, "Where did you learn that? Why did you do it that way?"

Most of my answers were the same. "That's how I was taught at school." At one point he said, "You do more things correctly than most catchers learn in a lifetime." Before I could even say "thank you," he turned and walked away.

Practices got boring sometimes. The only relief was that they sent me over to work with a set of pitchers who were coming off injuries. Two of them were on the major league roster and even though they were injured, they could still really bring it. It seemed as if all the pitchers were having a contest to see which one could throw the hardest.

One of the coaches told me; "kid you have very soft hands. Do you know how to pull a pitch?"

"Coach, I am not sure what you mean by pulling a pitch."

"Oh, yeah, I sometimes forget how old I am. Can you frame a pitch?" (to frame or pull a pitch, the catcher alters the position of the pitch so it will look better to the umpire and maybe be called a strike).

"Sure, but I was told not to do it here so the coaches could evaluate the pitchers better."

"Okay, do a few for me, alright?

So the coach would tell me what pitches to frame. He would nod at the pitcher and the pitcher would throw a near strike and I would frame it as it crossed the plate.

After a few minutes, the pitcher had reached his pitch count and was headed to the clubhouse. He said to me, "Thanks for the workout."

They sent me back to the minor league camp to finish out my day.

The drive back and forth to the house was nearly an hour and a quarter. It was an easy drive, but I was using my mom's car and that left her without a one. I talked with her later and we decided that it would be a great idea for me to get my own wheels.

I settled on a two-year-old pickup. I did have the Ford running by then but I did not favor driving it where it could get damaged.

Once the rookie season started, I began to stay in Lakeland. The night games made it more difficult to make the drive home while being tired, and return again the next day.

We began to have road games and they added to the confusion. Slowly I made the transition from my mom's place to a shared apartment in Lakeland. My roomy was the other rookie I had met on my first day in camp.

I was starting most of the games and the coaches would tell me what games they wanted me to frame pitches. They choose the games based on what umpires were behind the plate. About my fourth game in, I hit my first dinger. I was batting right-handed and hit it out to right center. It really felt good!

Out of boredom, I spent time on the phone with Bev, my mom and sometimes Jack. He would ask me how it was going and would give me encouragement and advice.

The conversations with Bev were different. We spent our time talking about her classes and how much we missed each other. We seemed to avoid any serious talk about our future as a couple.

A few days after signing, I left to join the Lakeland Tigers, the rookie class A team of the Detroit Tigers. The manager worked me into the lineup pretty much as soon as I stepped off of the bus.

Since I had played in Florida and had already played against many of the ballplayers, the transition for me was quick and easy.

In the sixth game of the year, I hit two home runs and had a third ball hit the base of the outfield wall. As I rounded the bases after my second homer, the fans began to chant, "Black Jack, Black Jack!" I couldn't help from smiling. The team had started out great. We were 14-2, and the clubhouse was a great place to be. It was a clubhouse of a bunch of young wild guys who loved playing baseball.

Prior to the next road trip, the GM for player development called me into his office and told me the club was moving me up to the Double AA club in Michigan. I would be the catcher for the Michigan Whitecaps. The team gave me two days off to get my stuff settled in Florida.

When I got back to Michigan I had forgotten how cold it could be in the late spring. My mom met me at Metro Airport and we drove over to the ballpark. She had been there a few days before and had set me up with an apartment.

I remember Jack telling me of the time he had stayed with a local couple to save a few bucks, so I realized how fortunate I was to have an apartment to live in.

The club was just finishing up a road trip and was due for a night game. I figured I would be able to make it there on time for the night game.

The Michigan White Caps baseball team manager was a former major league catcher and the Tigers wanted me to learn from him. For my first game, the manager had me sit with him and we discussed the flow of the game. It reminded me of my first college games with Uncle Jack.

The second game on the following night, he had me in the lineup as a DH. I did get a hit. A "seeing eye" single through the hole at short. As I got to first, I was thinking "they all look like line drives in the box scores."

As the season went on, I fell in with the other guys and the rhythm of the season. June slid into July, and then August. I was hitting okay, but not much for power. The pitchers were not giving me much to hit.

During the dog days of August, the pitcher began to tiresome and get impatient to end the games. They began to challenge me more and as they did so, my power hitting also increased without a drop off in batting average.

By the end of August, the Tigers were in third place and too many games back to make the playoffs. The Tigers then began calling up players from AAA Toledo. Each team was limited to a 40 man roster and most teams called players up, based on that rooster. Other players not on the 40 man roster can be called up if another player is on the injury list that ends their season. As luck would have it, one of the catchers broke his foot so the club called me up as insurance. I would be the third catcher.

Although it was only a three-hour drive from western Michigan, I could not sleep. So I started out before daylight. I drove into Detroit and arrived early in the morning. I had arrived before the clubhouse guy and the security guys would not let me in until he arrived.

At the time, I did not know it but the local paper had an article about me being called up. I found out after the game that many of my friends had bought tickets.

I knew my mom and grandparents were going to be there even though I had told them that the chances of me getting in any of the games before the season's end were slim to none.

The clubhouse manager had prepped a uniform with number 55 on the back. When I went up to get the uniform he asked me, "this number okay?"

"Sure! I am just glad I have a uniform to wear"

"Keep that attitude kid and you'll do fine."

The coaching staff assigned me to the bullpen. I would warm up the relief pitchers before they went into the game. Along with me, there was one other rookie in the pen. He was a big lefty that could really bring it on IF he could find the plate. As we were both rookies and not knowing anyone else, we sat together.

The game did not go well for the Tigers. They were three runs down in the third inning. That meant they would be into using the bullpen early.

They told "Lefty" to get loose prior to the eighth inning, and they told me to catch him. He was really quick and as fast as I had ever caught. His pitches all had movement. His fastball was a riser, which seemed to rise as it crossed the plate. When he kept the ball down, I began to frame the pitch. He and I were extremely nervous but we were just having too much fun to stop.

They called us both into the dugout between innings and told us that we'd both be going into the game in the ninth inning. Lefty and I found a place way at the end of the dugout and waited our turn. In the bottom of the ninth, we went in and began our warm-ups. Lefty was so nervous he could not find the plate. So before he finished his warm-ups, I went out and asked him if he had a date for dinner after the game?

He gave me a dumb ass look like "What?"

Then I told him "If he could not get the ball over the plate, his dinner was going to be back in Toledo." He just laughed at that one but it seemed to loosen him up a little.

The inning started and aside from tossing a few into the dirt, Lefty did fairly well. He struck out the first batter on a riser. He walked the second batter on six pitches and struck out the third batter with a slider down and low. He then got the final out when the batter hit a weak grounder to second base.

I was scheduled to be the fourth batter and was beginning to think about how the pitchers were working the hitters. I was on deck when the last out was made. The Tigers had gotten beat by Cleveland, 12-4.

During the remainder of September, I worked in the bullpen and got to pinch run in one game. We were on a short road trip and the "Skipper", (major league managers are sometimes referred to as Skipper by the ballplayers), told me he was going to put me in the game after the starting catcher had gotten one at-bat. The catcher got his at-bat in the third inning and Skip told me to suit up. I got my first at-bat in the fifth inning. The other team had one of their prized call-ups on the mound and he was doing well. He had only given up two hits thus far in the game and two walks.

I remember being nervous, but not like I had been when I had started college a few years ago. I figured I would be challenged right off the bat and I was right. I took the first pitch, a fastball right down the middle of the plate. Strike one! The second pitch was a slider down and in. Ball one!

The third pitch was another fastball down the middle. I put a good solid swing on the ball and I knew I had my first major league hit. A solid double to right center. I was on top of the world! We ended up winning the game 4-3 and I was able to get a sacrifice bunt down to advance a runner in the eighth inning. I was as happy as a clam! Ecstatic to say the least.

A few games later, I got my first home run. It was a long, high fly ball that hit the facing of the right-field second deck. I knew it might have been a fly out in many of the other stadiums, but in the box score in the newspaper, it would look like a line drive.

After the season ended, I went back to Florida and was able to go back to school and my classes.

Chapter 17

THE DOUBLE HEADER

Once Billy signed with the Tigers and the hoopla settled down, we all drifted back to our normal lives. I got back to coaching and teaching my classes at the college and doing my consultant work with the major league clubs. In addition to the Cubs, I had picked up another three baseball clubs. My one-time sedate life was getting complicated, to say the least.

Exploits of Billy's progression in pro-ball came from Beverly more than anyone else. And because Billy was considered an adopted son of the small college town in which I still lived, the local newspaper would run stories of his exploits.

I heard from Sharon that the Tigers were moving Billy up two rungs on the minor league ladder. He had gone from a middle-value prospect to the number one catching prospect. It reminded me of when I was playing in Iowa and was told that "Potential is a French word that means you have not done anything yet." So it would seem that Billy had plenty of potentials.

Billy went from the White Caps to Detroit. He sent his mom the ball that was his first major league hit. Sharon had the ball encased in one of the plastic ball containers and was saving all the news articles about his rise to the majors. She sounded like any proud mom would. I too was very proud of Billy and the progress he had made in just a few short years. I just wished that his dad could have been here to see it too. I had plenty of time to reflect on my great childhood friend and all the good times we had playing ball and just hanging out.

What I found interesting was the fans had also given him the nickname of "Black Jack." It was a carryover from when he played baseball for me in Florida.

Because Billy was no longer around, I worked on the old Ford by myself and began spending more time with Eddie. I was finding that I enjoyed the times we shared together. I began to ask Eddy about the time I had spent at Great Lakes. At first, Eddy was reluctant to talk about it because she knew the effect it could have on me. For me, I thought it was time for me to face my past in order to better deal with my future. We then began a ritual as we ate simple meals, lounging by the pool and sometimes riding to and from the college when our schedules permitted.

Beverly was there some of the time, but she was now so deep into her medical classes that when she was home, we hardly ever saw her.

At times, I found myself holding hands with Eddie when we went places. It seemed so natural. One evening we got a little closer and I realized I wanted us to get closer. However, I was reluctant to say anything because of the possibility of rejection. I knew in my gut that Eddie cared for me. It showed in her mannerisms towards me and the fact that she would sometimes initiate the hand holding and light touching. I could also tell in the manner in which she told me of my life at Great Lakes.

One evening I asked Eddie how she felt about me. She was very frank and told me that she loved me and wanted to see our relationship progress into something more. I agreed. After all these years of being single, I realized that I also wanted to see us progress beyond the hand holding stage. So out of the blue, I said; "I want to marry you, Eddie! I want more for us."

Eddie said; "Jack, we've had such a history with each other that goes way back through the years. The kids are all growing up and going off in their different directions and careers. It seemed like the day of having an empty nest was a long way off, but now I'm realizing it's just around the corner. The thought of growing old with you gives me comfort. And, I realize that I want to marry you too Jack. So, now what do you suggest?"

After thinking for a minute, I said "Let's tell the kids and we'll plan a date when everyone can be here for the wedding. How does that sound?" "Yes! That sounds great! I often wondered if you would ever get around to asking."

Once we got our collective heads together, we decided that the Thanksgiving weekend would probably work out for everyone. Billy would be home and serve as my Best Man. Beverly would be on a ten-day break from school and she would be the Maid of Honor for her mom. Sharon and the folks from Michigan would all be down for the winter by then too. We set the date for the wedding on the Saturday after Thanksgiving. Eddie and Carol got right on it, to plan all the details.

Billy was staying in Lakeland at his condo and commuting back and forth to school. The trip for him was less than an hour and a half. Billy ended up coming a few days early when the school break started and told me he had news that he wanted to share with me, but wanted to tell his mom first.

When Sharon arrived in early November, she, Eddie, Beverly and Billy all huddled together for a few minutes and then the shrieking began.

I casually walked over to the pool area and Eddie told me; "Billy and Beverly have decided to get married too and guess what? We are having a double wedding!"

Ever the practical one, I asked if the addition of more guests would be covered by the food and other items we already had ordered for the party?

"Not a problem, I'll get on the phone and tell the caterer to plan for 25 or so more people. We should have plenty of room here to expand the seating arrangements."

So the die was cast and I did not have to do anything but just show up. Oh, and to get my family down here. For that, I would rely on Jay, Jody and my sister June. She pitched in to have the Michigan clan to make the trip so my family was able to attend. It was great to see them all. Even my older brother had lost that tough Marine look and was looking more and more like the successful businessman he had become.

Billy and I partnered up and were standing at the altar waiting for the love of our lives. Two very happy fellows. My brother Jay did the honors and walked the ladies down the aisle one on each arm. That rat had a smile on his ugly mug from ear to ear.

The wedding went very well. I was extremely happy. I guess I hadn't realized how much I loved Eddie until I saw her standing next to me at the altar. I reflected on all the years I had known my sweet Eddie and all the things she had done for me. Now, all I could think about was how much I wanted to please her.

The guests all had a great time and stayed till the wee hours of the next morning. One of the big surprises of the day was that Sharon had asked the GM from the Tigers, Ron Meredith to be her date for the evening. Even a blind man could see the feeling that those two had for each other.

Chapter 18

EXTRA INNINGS
<u>EDDIE & JACK</u>

Jack and I were a couple now. Aside from being married, not much had changed. We had become best friends before our marriage, and our friendship grew even stronger afterward. We shared the same values and the love of our children.

Even though Jack had no children of his own, he thought of Billy as a son and treated him as he did all the young ballplayer he coached. It was never a surprise to see a strange young new face at our dinner table. Many were away from home for the first time and just needed to sit down and enjoy a friendly meal in a family setting. I found that I enjoyed having those young folks at dinner as much as Jack did.

The Love Bug was still in the air. A few months after our wedding, my son Tom and Jack's niece Nicole said they too were planning a wedding to be held in Michigan, in the Spring. Nicole wanted to make sure her Grandma and all her cousins could be there to attend. The only question would be if Billy and Beverly could make it due to spring training in Lakeland. Nicole and Tom's wedding coincided with his budding medical career.

Through my own life experience, I had a great understanding of doctors and their medical careers after being married to one for nearly 20 years. My hope was that Tom learned some things by experiencing some of the challenges through his years growing up and that he would be a better husband and father that his father had been. Secretly I was elated to be able to show off my new family to the ex.

After being married for a short time, I began to notice that Jack paid very little attention to his finances. He paid his bills when they came in the mail, however, he seemed to get a few late notices. Some of which he had previously paid. So we decided I needed to look into his accounts. After a few months, we decided it was a good idea that I had done that and we decided it was best to keep his separate from mine. I was amazed at the amount of assets he had accumulated over the years because he always had lived so modestly.

Sharon and the Carters became interested in selling their company and had a ready customer in Jay, who was already a minority shareholder. Jack was trying to decide between selling his shares to Jay or just hanging on to them. When he asked me my thoughts, I told him, "Honey you already have enough money in the bank and do not need to have more cash sitting around doing nothing. Just stay with Jay as a silent partner."

Jack and I both continued to work at the University and Jack took on more teaching assignments to get himself ready for retirement from coaching. You could see the transformation in Jack as he eased into a professor's role at the college. Jack was a natural teacher. He had an easy, entertaining way about him that put his students at ease and in a learning mode. I was not surprised that he made the decision to teach full time.

My previous thoughts were that Jack would more likely die in the Coach's Box while waving a runner home. There was no way we'd ever get Jack to stop coaching, I thought. It was his lifelong passion and I could see it gave him such great joy to teach whenever he had the opportunity.

It was about that time that the Consulting he had begun with the Cubs expanded to other major league clubs. The clubs wanted Jack to act as a part-time instructor for their organization. Not for the players, but for their coaches and front office people who dealt with the players.

At first he didn't seem to know what value he could add to the clubs, However, he got into the swing of it after he gave his first talk. It wasn't long after that, word got around and he was in demand with a few other clubs. Jack was in his glory! He was so busy and so happy helping others to develop their skills. I just stood back and watched him glow. He really was a very humble, yet remarkable man.

SHARON

I had always thought I would never fall in love again. In my mind, I would always be in love with Will. I had never known another man who had touched my heart as he did. And there was Billy, so much like his father, yet so different. I had dedicated my existence to my family. I needed to ensure that Billy could be on his own one day and that Mom and Dad Carter would always be comfortable. Then one day, I woke up realizing that the others in my life had achieved what I had always hoped for them. In the years following Will's death in Vietnam, I had dated some, however, I could just not get serious about anyone.

When Billy signed with the Tigers though, I found I was intrigued by Ron Meredith the GM of the Tigers. One day, I found myself wanting to discuss minor details of Billy's contract. The odd thing was Ron was willing to meet with me to discuss the details also. Although, we never did make any changes to the actual contract. Those meetings became a casual lunch once in a while, just to talk baseball.

We'd also meet sometimes at various fields in the Detroit area when Ron would do follow up scouting for a local ballplayer. I adored the fact that he would ask my opinion about the team and appreciated my insight on the player's demeanor.

Those casual lunches went from that to holding hands and a planned get together. Ron's wife had divorced him years before because he spent too much time on the job. Funny thing was, I enjoyed spending time with him on the job. We were just getting serious when the news of the two weddings came to light. Both Ron and I were so happy that Billy was getting married. For me, because that meant grandchildren someday and for Ron, because as he put it; "married ballplayers were more stable."

One evening as we watched a Tiger game, Ron asked me to marry him. I was stunned. I didn't know how to answer him. I just looked at him with a thousand questions going through my head: Like what about this, what about that and on and on. His smile at me warmed my heart. I could tell that smile meant; "Why worry about all those things?" It had been many years since a man made me smile. How could ever I say "No" to that? I realized, it was time. So along with that winning smile, Ron said; "So does your smile mean yes?"

Ron took out a ring and asked me for my hand. Up to this point, I had not spoken a word. Ron opened a small jewelry box and put the ring on my finger. It was beautiful. The diamonds were arranged in the

Tiger old English D. I said "Yes!" Then right there in the suite, we kissed and all the people we were with began to applaud.

A few weeks later we officially announced our engagement. We first sat down with Mom and Dad Carter to talk to them about it. It was a little difficult until Mom said, "Shar it is way past time you moved on in your life. Will has been gone a very long time. Please move on. We all want that for you. And Ron, you better treat our girl good or you will hear from us."

There were hugs all around and a few tears too. We called Billy and he just laughed. He told me that the word had already gotten out and the guys were asking him to put in a good word with "The Boss," his future Step Dad.

BILLY

The second season with the "Big Club" was great for me, but not so much for the team. I ended up taking over the major catching duties. Our starting catcher's legs finally broke down just before the All-Star break and went on the 30-day disabled list. The remainder of the year as the starting catcher went by in a blur. There was so much to learn. Each pitcher I caught for had different quirks in their deliveries and personalities. I had not realized how much each pitcher relied on their catcher for almost everything. It was like having 13 younger brothers. All of the brother's worried about the smallest things. I began to realize I was as much a therapist as an athlete. I began to rely on some of the older fellows for support. I guess I was also learning that I could not carry the team alone and I too needed help. The year ended for us at 162 games. There would be no playoffs for us this year.

Later that fall, Bev and I had our first baby. A little-redheaded girl we named after her mom. No, not Edwina. We used her mom's middle name, Marie first, then Edwina.

My career took off after my second year and the big wild lefty found the plate and we won our division for the first time in years. However, we lost the series to St. Louis. All the players were a little ticked off and vowed to win it all the following season.

The next year, we did win it all and came close the following two seasons as well! I was again having fun playing ball. The younger guys were maturing and were less of a burden on me. That let me concentrate more on my offense. In retrospect, I had an outstanding year at the plate and made my first all-star team.

We were always in the hunt for a series bid each year that I played and finally did win it again in my last year. Like all catchers, my legs got heavy and I did play some first base and was a Designated Hitter in some of the games near the end of my career.

Somewhere along the line, my beautiful wife gave birth to two more babies. Both boys. One dark like me and the other a redhead like his mom. She was also able to fit in her schooling and finally became the doctor she always wanted to be. I will be forever proud of her for her accomplishments. She is the true leader in our family.

Eventually, Bev and I discussed a retirement plan for me. We both knew I could not play forever and we needed to focus on the next phase of our life. Bev was working at the local hospital in Florida and there was no way I would consider uprooting her and the kids. One of my true joys was being able to take my family to watch daddy at work. The boys loved being around the other ballplayers and seemed to have career plans to follow in dad's footsteps.

We both thought that I should retire after the season and skip the farewell tour that some players had done. I made sure the club knew of my plans before I retired so that they could plan ahead for the amateur draft and free agency. Then, one day it was over. It had been nearly 25 years for me to fall in love with the game of baseball, first as a smart ass 15-year old, to a tired mature man. What a great career.

EPILOG

COOPERSTOWN, NEW YORK BASEBALL HALL OF FAME INDUCTION CEREMONIES

<u>William (Black Jack) Carter</u>
<u>Catcher: Detroit Tigers</u>

Good morning, Ladies, Gentlemen and a very special good morning to my Mom, Grandma, my Wife, and our Children, who are all here at Cooperstown today to share this very special day!

First, I would like to thank all the folks who voted for me and those who bestowed this great honor to me. As many as you know, I lost my Father before I knew him. My Mom, Grandma, and Grandpa raised me and instilled the values that I have today.

As a ballplayer, I was fortunate to be raised in Detroit and play my professional career in the city that I love. I was also very fortunate to have a very supportive ball club and outstanding teammates. However, I was also extremely fortunate to be blessed with a man who was not only my Coach but was my second father and mentors all of my life. Many of you know Jack Tyler. What many of you do not know, was the personal sacrifices that he had made in his life.

Jack was a Triple-A ballplayer when he was drafted into the Army during the height of the Vietnam War. Because of a debilitating injury, he was unable to follow his dream in baseball. However, he made it possible for other young men to follow their dreams. I, along with Bob Bernard, another student and ballplayer mentored by Coach Jack are in the hall now. In addition, five other current major league ballplayers were also mentored by Coach Jack and if rumors are right there are more in Coach Jack's pipeline.

The "Hall of Fame" has honored me with the opportunity to be inducted among the greatest of men who played the game we all love. It was Coach Jack who instilled that love in me and a true passion for the game.

Therefore, it is my recommendation that the "Hall" would consider this, for future inductees as well, by creating a special category for great leaders like Coach Jack.

Given the contributions Coach Jack and other inspiring coaches have made from behind the scenes, it's my proposal that the Hall Of Fame would consider this honor for the Great Men who contributed to the game, by mentoring, coaching and supporting the great game of baseball. And so, I end my allotted few minutes by saying; "Thank you Cooperstown, Mom, Dad, Grandma, Grandpa and my Special Thanks to my "Uncle Jack."

Billy Jack Carter went on to coach and manage in the major leagues. Billy eventually retired to Florida some years later and can still be seen roaming the minor league facilities of the Detroit Tigers. He also spends time assisting with his old college baseball team.

Jack "The Coach" Tyler: Builder of Game

The Hall of Fame eventually created a special area in the "Hall" for folks like Jack. Jack was one of the first people enshrined under that category. "Builders of Game." During his induction, Jack was so emotional, he had his friend Billy Jack, read his thank you speech. A few lines from his speech were as follows: "I am a happy man today, and yet I grieve for those who are not able to be here today. My special friend Will, his father Bill Sr., and my own father, These men, who inspired me and who will always be in my heart."

Never one who paid attention to money, upon his death, Jack donated his legacy to the inner City of Detroit and his adopted Florida city for youth baseball and softball facilities. In addition, he set up a scholarship program for his siblings and their children, so that they could all attend college.

THE PLAYERS:

Sharon Carter-Meredith: Tiger Den Mother

Sharon was the proud Mom of her son Billy. She also became the proud and happy Grandma to all five of her grandchildren. In addition she also took under her wing, many of the young ball players who were away from home for the first time. She was responsible for creating the *"Will Carter Residence,"* a housing facility for young players and their families.

Eddie Paulson Tyler

Eddie was the proud mother of Tom and Beverly. Both doctors. She and Jack had a long and happy marriage. Eddie enjoyed watching Jack work with the many young players that came through the university. In their later years Eddie was elated that Jack's past and experiences in Vietnam seemed to fade until they became fond memories of Jack and his buddies and the clowning they did at the base camp.

Jody & Carol Tyler: Entrepreneurs

Jody and Carol were able to make wise investments in real estate and through the years were able to buy up many of the failing orange grove farms in Florida. They were future thinkers and assisted in building multiple condo developments which are the norm in Florida and played a major role in the development of many small cities all along the l-75 corridor.

Jay Tyler:
Retired Marine / Business Man:

Jay and his silent partner Jack increased the business again and again so it became a leader in worldwide manufacturing. Jay developed into a national leader and world figure, in addition he served on the National Manufacturers Counsel under two US Presidents. In later years, it came to light that Jay had been among the first Marines to enter the City of Hue during that historic battle in Vietnam and had rescued nearly a dozen young Marines trapped in the middle of the city square. He had repeatedly gone into the line of fire and physically dragged the Marines back to safety. He himself had been hit twice by small arms fire and had numerous holes in his protective vest. Jay was awarded the Navy Cross during his service and never told a soul about his exploits while in Vietnam.

In his senior years, Coach Jack,
shared his love of baseball by coaching
young ball players both on and off the fields,
until one night, he quietly passed away in his sleep.

Jack's funeral was held at the
National Military Cemetery in Sarasota, Florida,
with full Military Honors.

On Jack's headstone is engraved:
"The Coach"

Jan Reed Bales

ABOUT THE AUTHOR

Jan Reed Bales is a retired automotive engineer who has had the outline of this story bouncing around in his head for years. "The Coach" is his first attempt at writing.

Much of this story is close to factual and is a compilation and reflection of his own life experiences, plus those of his close friends who have related their experiences to him as well.

Jan currently does volunteer work at the Great Lakes National Cemetery in Holly, Michigan. His background includes many years as a youth baseball and softball coach.

TO CONTACT THE AUTHOR:
balesjan43@gmail.com

ADDITIONAL BOOKS BY
JAN REED BALES:

ACES WILD SERIES
Misfire - 2018

Made in the USA
Monee, IL
02 June 2021